Book Six
The Trail of the Ghost Bunny

Linda Joy Singleton

Albert Whitman & Company
Chicago, Illinois

Library of Congress Cataloging-in-Publication
data is on file with the publisher.

LC record available at https://lccn.loc.gov/2018003936

Text copyright © 2018 by Linda Joy Singleton
First published in the United States of America in
2018 by Albert Whitman & Company
ISBN 978-0-8075-1392-7

Printed in the United States of America
10 9 8 7 6 5 4 3 2 1 LB 22 21 20 19 18

Cover art copyright © 2018 by Tracy Bishop
Interior illustrations and hand lettering by Jordan Kost
Design by Ellen Kokontis

For more information about Albert Whitman & Company,
visit our website at www.albertwhitman.com.

Dedicated to my talented and wonderful BC
friends: Danna Smith and Linda Whalen

Chapters

- Chapter 1 -
Ghost Story

"It was a shivery, stormy night when I heard the death bells," the old woman says ominously, wringing sorrow out of each syllable. She swivels her wheelchair away from the curious stares of my siblings to point a bony finger directly at me. "I was the same age as you."

Me? I try not to look surprised as I grip the edge of the packing box I'm using as a chair. I can't imagine this ancient woman ever being thirteen. She's shriveled like a dried potato, with scraggly wisps of gray hair dangling down her frail shoulders. I only met her moments ago, when our realtor, Mr. Dansbury, arrived at our new house. When we'd bought the place, Mr. Dansbury told my parents that it came with some sort of secret inheritance, and now he was here to tell them about it. He'd introduced the old woman as his aunt Philomena, and asked us kids to sit with her while he talked with my parents.

"Aunt Philomena used to play in this house as a child, so she wanted to visit," Mr. Dansbury had explained. He rolled his aunt's wheelchair into the living room before disappearing behind a closed door with my parents.

I longed to follow and find out what we'd inherited when we'd bought this old house. When I told my Curious Cat Spy Club friends Leo and Becca there was a secret inheritance, we tried to guess what it could be. Logical Leo guessed a classic jalopy car since the house was built in the 1920s. Becca thought it was vintage jewelry or clothes. And I hoped for something thrilling like a cryptic map to buried treasure.

And just when the secret was *finally* being revealed, I was stuck babysitting an old lady.

But it turns out the old lady has secrets of her own to share. When she smiled slyly and offered to tell us a ghost story, even my three older siblings took a break from unpacking boxes to listen.

"Death bells don't sound like ordinary bells," Aunt Philomena continues, her intense gaze sweeping from my brother to my twin sisters, then back to me. "They harmonize so sweetly, I thought I was listening to a symphony of angels. But later I found out it was the opposite. When the death bells ring, someone is going to die."

I glance over at my siblings, expecting them to roll their eyes because there's no such thing as death bells. But Kenya and Kiana huddle close on the faded velvet couch, both bug-eyed, while Kyle munches potato chips with an intense expression, like he's watching a horror movie.

"The wealthiest girl from school, Caroline Olivianne Whitney, invited me to her slumber party in this very house." Philomena sweeps her arm toward the high ceiling. "This room was called the parlor, and there used to be a crystal chandelier that sparkled like diamonds. It was the grandest house I ever saw, shining like a palace by the river." She pauses and looks around, fear in her eyes. "And it was haunted."

"Our new home is haunted?" Kiana hugs a couch pillow.

"Like with *real* ghosts?" Kenya adds, grabbing a pillow to hug too.

"Ghosts aren't real," my brother says in a know-it-all voice.

"'All houses wherein men have lived and died are haunted houses'—that's a Longfellow quote." Philomena's thin lips twist into a wicked smile, and I realize she's just trying to scare us.

Fortunately, I'm not easily scared. As the Spy Specialist in the Curious Cat Spy Club, I've trained myself to analyze clues and sort truth from lies. Still, it's fun to hear a ghost story, and I grab a handful of chips from Kyle's bowl.

"That fateful night still haunts me." Philomena sips tea from the coffee cup we were lucky to find in the jumble of our moving boxes. She puckers her mouth as if the tea—or her memory—is bitter.

"What happened?" I ask, dying to know but uneasy too. How will I be able to sleep in my new home if it really *is* haunted?

"I had a lovely day celebrating Caroline's birthday with girls from school," she says in such a low voice that I scoot closer. "Caroline was the only child of a divorced father who gave her anything she wanted. We enjoyed pony rides, a magic show, and triple-layered chocolate cake. Everywhere Caroline went, her pet bunny Trixie hopped along too. Caroline loved her bunny so much that her father gave her a stuffed toy bunny with white and black floppy ears handmade to look exactly like Trixie. And all us girls at the party received a similar stuffed toy as a party favor. I still have mine." A wisp of a smile crosses her face then sinks into a scowl. "But the happy birthday party turned into a tragic deathday."

My sisters gasp, but I know they're not scared. I'm not either because it's just a story. I play along, though, and let my eyes go wide like I'm afraid.

"Late that night while the other girls were sleeping," the old lady continues dramatically, "I awoke to the sound of bells. When I looked over at Caroline's bed, it was empty. Caroline, Trixie, and even the toy bunny were gone. And the strange bells kept ringing." A lemony sage aroma wafts around the room as she sips her tea. "Where was I? Oh, yes, the empty bed. I thought Caroline must be looking for the bells, so I slipped on a robe, grabbed a flashlight, and followed the sounds. But the bells echoed from all directions. I was scared and started to turn back, when I heard a thump-thump—and then I saw the bunny."

"Trixie?" Kyle guesses as he grabs more chips.

"I thought so, except it was transparent." She shivers. "It hopped down the staircase and vanished—like a ghost. I never saw the bunny or Caroline again."

"Ohmygod!" Kiana's hands fly to her cheeks. "What happened to them?"

"No one knows for sure." Philomena shakes her head solemnly. "But the next morning, one of Caroline's shoes was found near the river. Everyone was sure she'd drowned, except her father. He insisted she'd been kidnapped. He shut up the house, and some people say he traveled the world searching for Caroline. When he returned for short visits, he was seen carrying boxes from faraway countries into the house. Rumors spread that he was collecting priceless treasures. Decades later, an illness brought him home to stay, until one night the death bells called for him too," the old woman finishes with a sigh. "He died alone, and no treasure was ever found. The house sat empty for years until new owners transformed it into a bed-and-breakfast, naming it Down the Rabbit Hole Inn. And on stormy nights, guests claimed to hear bells and see a ghostly bunny hopping on the staircase."

My brother rubs his stubbly chin, frowning. "Has anyone else died here?"

"Oh yes. Many." Philomena nods a bit too enthusiastically. "But not since the bed-and-breakfast closed down. No one has lived here for two years...until now." She flashes a wicked grin, as if she expects us to tremble in fear.

If I'm trembling, it's because I'm excited by the rumor of treasure. *Treasure!* I taste the word on my lips and it's delicious. I love mysteries and secrets. My CCSC club mates will be here soon, and I can't wait to tell them about this. Searching for treasure could be a fun mystery to solve. Of course, the goal of the CCSC is to help animals. Does a ghost bunny count?

Where could the treasure be hidden?

I've been in every room in our house and only found dust, cobwebs, and mouse droppings (eww!). If something valuable was hidden here, why hasn't anyone found it?

My curiosity mounts as I gaze around the room. Our unpacked boxes surround a meager assortment of old furniture that belonged to the previous owner. Most of it is broken, ripped, and destined for the junk pile. My parents warned us when we bought this house that we'd have to work hard to fix it up. Serious understatement. After a week of sweeping, scrubbing, and painting, only a few rooms are livable. Even worse, only one toilet flushes—and it's on the third floor. Still I don't complain, because, not long ago, my family didn't have a home at all. We were split up between friends and family. I'm glad we're back together—even if living here feels like camping.

"*No!* Absolutely not!" My dad's voice explodes and footsteps thunder down the hall. Dad storms past the living room. Mom rushes after him with Mr. Dansbury close behind, a folder clutched in his hand.

While my siblings and Aunt Philomena gape in surprise, I spring to my feet and race out of the room to find out what's going on. My parents and the realtor face off in the foyer. Dad's cheeks are crimson with fury.

"Kevin, let's discuss this!" Mom says, as she tugs on Dad's sleeve.

"I refuse to sign the paper." Dad purses his lips stubbornly. "I can't agree to such ridiculous rules."

"We can't back out now," Mom insists.

"She's right." The realtor wipes sweat from his

balding head. "When you bought this house, you became the owners of everything on this property on the condition that you accept a bequest. You're legally bound to the contract rules."

"Not if I don't sign the blasted papers! I won't be told what to do in my own house. Mr. Dansbury, please leave." Dad gestures to the ornately carved front door. "Our business is over."

"Be reasonable, Kevin," Mom says in a soothing tone that can calm wild animals—and my angry father.

"The bequest is *not* reasonable!" Dad rubs his forehead, his expression softening. "Katherine, our dream is to eventually restore this house into a bed-and-breakfast inn. Our house needs to be orderly and sanitary. This bequest will cause chaos."

"It won't be a problem. The kids will help—especially Kelsey." Mom turns toward me. "Isn't that right, Kelsey?"

"Um...yes?" I say uncertainly. *What am I agreeing to?*

"See? There's nothing to worry about," Mom assures Dad. "We can still turn our home into a wonderful B and B. Guests will come from far away to enjoy your culinary talents."

"I hope you're right." Sighing, Dad turns back to the realtor. "I'm not happy about this. You should have told us about this sooner."

"I had to follow legal procedure and couldn't reveal the bequest until now." Mr. Dansbury stands taller, squaring his slim shoulders. "But I don't understand why you're so distressed. It's small and harmless."

"And it will be no trouble at all." Mom slips her arm around Dad. "I promise you, everything will be fine. Go ahead. Sign the paper."

Dad's shoulders sag as he holds out his hand to the realtor.

"Excellent!" Mr. Dansbury whips out a paper and pen quickly, as if he's afraid Dad will change his mind. Once my father signs, the realtor folds the paper and tucks it in his pocket. Then he grins at my parents. "Now let's go get the cage."

- Chapter 2 -
Strange Inheritance

I follow Dad, Mom, and Mr. Dansbury outside, shivering at the word *cage*. I've had some bad experiences with cages—once I was even trapped in one. As I cross the porch, I glance over at the detached garage on the side of our new house. Although weathered with age, it looks like an ordinary garage. But not long ago it was a criminal hideout crammed with cages of poorly treated dogs—until Becca, Leo, and I followed clues that led to their rescue.

We also rescued my mom from a scary situation. You'd think Mom would never want to see this house again—but it was her idea to buy it. Practical Mom couldn't resist a good deal. Besides, it's not easy finding an affordable home large enough for a family of six, plus my small cat, Honey, and our large dog, Handsome. During the renovations, Handsome is staying with my grandmother, but my kitten sleeps with me in the second-floor bedroom I'm temporarily sharing with my sisters.

"Can I have some help with this cage?" Mr. Dansbury calls out, car keys jangling from his fingers.

What sort of creature have we inherited? I wonder as I hurry over to the dark-gray SUV parked on the cracked concrete driveway. When the realtor lifts the back hatch, sunshine glints off the wire of a large cage. Something moves inside.

Mr. Dansbury leans into the van, blocking my view. I shift around him, curious to see inside the cage. I guess it holds a lizard, snake, or alligator because of Dad's attitude—Dad hates reptiles.

When Mr. Dansbury lifts the cage, I stare in surprise. Definitely not a slimy or scaly reptile. Tucked in a wire hutch is the cutest bunny I've ever seen. It's about the size of my hand, spotted brown and white, with adorable floppy ears. And I immediately fall in love.

I grin at Mr. Dansbury. "Boy or girl?"

"Girl." Mr. Dansbury pulls out the large cage, bags of rabbit food, litter, and a litter box. This tiny bunny comes with a lot of luggage.

"How sweet," Mom coos. "She's smaller than I expected."

Dad scowls. "She may be cute, but rodents are not sanitary."

"A rabbit isn't a rodent," Mom says with an amused smile. She's an animal control officer and knows a lot about animals. "They eat vegetables, not meat."

"Quite right," Mr. Dansbury says as he balances the large cage in his arms. "She's very neat and good about using her litter box."

"She'd better stay out of my kitchen," Dad warns, "or she's hasenpfeffer."

I don't know what hasenpfeffer is and don't want to. "Dad, she won't go into your kitchen," I assure him, trying to copy Mom's calming voice. "I'll be happy to take care of her. She'll stay locked in her cage most of the time in my room."

"Actually...no." Mr. Dansbury purses his lips uneasily.

"Huh?" I blink at the realtor. "What do you mean?"

He pulls at his collar as if suddenly warm although it's a cool May morning. "The bunny has her own room with a pet door, so she has complete run of the house like she did before her owner died," he explains in an apologetic tone.

Now I know why Dad is so angry. He only allowed me to have an inside cat because I promised to keep Honey with me or in my bedroom. And I remember Becca saying rabbits live about ten years. This one looks young, so she could be hopping around our house for a long time.

"I assure you she won't be any trouble," Mr. Dansbury adds hastily. "I've been caring for her since the previous owner passed away."

"Did you give her free run of *your* house?" Dad asks sarcastically.

"No. But I didn't have a pet door like you do." Mr. Dansbury shifts the cage in his arms so he can click his key remote to lock the SUV. "Let's go inside. This is getting heavy."

As I carry a bag of litter, questions ping-pong in my head, until one slips out. "Why did the previous owner leave her bunny to us?" I ask the realtor. "I mean, she couldn't know who would buy her house."

"It's a long tradition for the Down the Rabbit Hole B and B to have a pet rabbit in the house. There have been several owners, and they all kept a pet bunny like a mascot." He pauses to shift the cage in his arms. "The inn was a thriving business until the last owner died, and his wife closed the B and B. She lived alone for a long time with only bunnies for company."

"There were *more* bunnies?" Dad looks horrified.

"Yes, but not at the same time," the realtor explains. "Whenever one bunny died, the inn owners got a new bunny. This little girl is almost three years old—and she's the smartest of all the B and B bunnies."

"Does she like to be held?" I ask, eager to cuddle her. Dad may think a bunny in our house is a catastrophe, but I feel like we won the lottery. I can't wait to tell Becca and Leo.

"She's very friendly," the realtor assures us, catching his breath before climbing up the steep porch steps. "But she's a clever escape artist. The number one rule for this bunny's care is to always keep the front and back doors closed so she doesn't go outside. It's too dangerous because of predators like foxes and hawks. The estate will give your family a generous bonus for bunny care. Keep her safe, and treat her like a family member."

Dad glowers, but I flash Mr. Dansbury a big grin.

"I will," I promise, gazing into the shining black eyes of our new family member.

I'm climbing the stairs as another question pops into my head. I turn back to the realtor. "Mr. Dansbury, you never told us the bunny's name."

"Didn't I?" He chuckles. "Why, of course, it's Trixie."

A short while later, I hear the whirl of bike tires. Becca pedals over our bumpy driveway, her leopard-spotted scarf flying behind her.

"Sorry I'm late," she says as she hops off her bike, leaning it against the side of the porch steps. She's wearing purple leggings with tiny black paw prints climbing up the sides and a lavender *I ♥ Animals* t-shirt. The heart is shaped by drawings of animals. Becca always wears the coolest clothes.

"You're not late, but Leo is." I glance over her shoulder to the thick line of trees shadowing the private road leading to our new home. "Have you heard from him?"

"He just texted," she says, patting the phone-sized lump in her shirt pocket. "He was flying drones with the sheriff and had to drop them off at his house before coming here. But he's on his way." Becca throws up her hands with a groan. "It's bad enough Sheriff Fischer is dating my mother, but now he's best buddies with Leo. I can't get away from him."

"Well I think it's great he's hanging out with Leo," I say. "Leo never complains, but I know he misses his father since the separation. And Sheriff Fischer seems impressed with Leo's drones."

"He should be impressed. Leo is a genius." Becca suddenly whirls around and points. "Here he comes now."

I turn just as Leo zooms up on his gyro-board. The robotic skateboard is one of Leo's inventions, and it's faster and smoother than riding a bike. Whenever Becca, Leo, and I ride around Sun Flower searching for lost pets, Leo is usually in the lead.

Leo looks nice in casual jeans and a T-shirt instead of his usual button-down shirt with formal black pants. Last month, we went to a school dance together. It wasn't a date because we're just good friends, but I get a happy, jumpy feeling when he's around.

"Sorry I'm four minutes late." He props up his gyro-board beside our bikes. "What did I miss?"

"Nothing. I was just getting ready to show Becca our new family member," I add mysteriously.

"OMG!" Becca's hands fly to her cheeks. "Did your parents adopt a baby?"

"No," I say, laughing. "Four kids in our family are enough. This little girl has paws and floppy ears. She came with the house. And she's adorable!"

As I lead my friends around boxes and up the stairs to the second floor, I tell them all about the bequest.

"Dad really freaked out when he found out we'd inherited a bunny." I sniff the air. "But I smell cinnamon and chocolate so he must be baking through his anger. I love it when Dad does therapy baking."

Becca licks her glossy lips. "I hope he shares."

"He always does. Come meet Trixie." I open the door to my temporary bedroom. "My sisters and I are bunking here until the rooms we've chosen for ourselves are painted and repaired. I had no idea this room belonged to Trixie. I guess that explains why it's in better shape than the others. I thought the pet door was for a cat or dog—not a pampered bunny."

I lead Becca and Leo past the three beds that fill most of the room to the back where stacked boxes are pushed against one wall and a rabbit hutch against the other. Trixie's litter box is in a corner beside my cat's litter box. I glance around, expecting Honey to be curled up on my pillow or in her kitty bed. Instead, she's perched on a box near Trixie's cage, staring at the sleeping bunny.

"Honey is curious about our new family member." I rub my orange kitten below her neck. She purrs but keeps staring at the bunny as if hypnotized.

"Be careful," Becca warns. "Some cats eat bunnies."

"Honey wouldn't hurt anything. She just wants to play with Trixie."

"Yeah. Right." Becca twists a loose strand from her ponytail. "But keep them apart until you know for sure."

Leo tilts his head, studying the bunny. "Her size is unusually minuscule."

"I think she's a dwarf Holland lop," Becca says as she peers into the cage. "We take in lots of rabbits after Easter every year because people buy a cute pet like they're toys, then they get bored and abandon them. We don't get many this small though. She's adorable. Can I hold her?"

"Sure." I slide the latch and the wire door opens.

As Becca reaches for the bunny, music shrills from her pocket.

"A text…but that's odd." Becca glances at her phone with a puzzled expression. "Why is she—"

"Trixie!" I interrupt with a shriek. *"No!"*

Everything happens so fast. The bunny jumps from her cage and bounces off beds to reach the door. I'd remembered to shut the door but forgot about the small pet door that Trixie pushes through.

"Get back here!" I'm yelling as Becca, Leo, and I race out of the room in pursuit of the bad bunny.

"She's going down the stairs," Leo calls, already ahead of us since he's the fastest runner. "I'll catch her."

I hear a scream from one of my sisters and guess that Trixie has reached the living room. I keep running, taking two stairs at a time. Voices raise. Oh no! One of them is Dad's. When I reach the front door, my parents and siblings are staring at the open front door. I want to yell at whoever left the door open, but I'm too busy running after Leo. He's racing toward the weeded patch of land that used to be a garden. I hurry after him, with Becca right behind me.

"Leo!" I catch up to him, breathing fast. "Where is she?"

"Around the back of the house." He picks up his pace, so I run faster too.

Becca trails behind us, but I don't wait for her. All I can think about is finding Trixie. My worry increases when I turn the corner and see the mountain of berry bushes that separate the house from the rushing river. Clouds cut off the sun, and I shiver, wishing I'd worn my jacket. But there's no time to go back. I must find Trixie, or a wild animal might find her first.

"She went into the pump house." Becca points to a small building near the edge of the property where berry bushes tangle down to the river.

"She's trapped," I say in relief. "There's only one door so she can't get out."

"She must be terrified," Becca says sympathetically. "Poor little bunny. I'll go inside and get her."

Leo nods. "I'll check around the back to make sure there aren't any holes she can escape through."

"And I'll guard the door," I add, moving in front of the doorway.

As I listen to Becca speak softly to the bunny, my gaze slides beyond the berry bushes to the rushing river far below. On an outcropping of rocks by the shore, a shadow moves. A small person, probably a kid my age, kneels beside the water, holding a long stick. No, not a stick, I realize as clouds shift and sunlight glints off the object. I stare curiously, trying to understand what I'm seeing.

The person—a girl, I can see now—turns suddenly toward me. The stick-like object in her hand glints like a golden wand, as if she's magical and casting a spell. Her long red braid swishes as she whips around to look directly at me.

In a flash, she vanishes into the bushes.

And the river rushes on as if she were never there.

- Chapter 3 -
Tricky Trixie

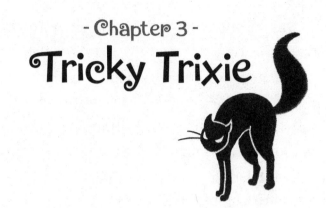

"Bad bunny!" Becca croons in a sweet voice as she cuddles Trixie in her arms.

"Thank goodness you caught her," I say. My gaze returns to the river below. Where did the girl go? There's no path, only prickly bushes so sharp and thick that anyone would be crazy to try to go through them.

Leo comes up beside me. "What are you staring at?"

I shield my eyes from the rising sun and squint at the rushing river. "Someone was standing by those big rocks. A girl."

"Seriously? How could anyone get down there?" Becca tilts her head to peer past the dense bushes.

"The cliff is too steep and covered with thorny bushes."

"There could be a path leading here from further down the river." Leo rubs his chin thoughtfully. "Or perhaps she came by boat."

"Do you see a boat? I don't. And the way she vanished was weird—like the berry bushes swallowed her." I stare at the impassable tangle of bushes. "And that's not the weirdest part."

"There's more?" Becca asks, stroking the bunny's head as we walk back to the house.

"She was holding something that I thought was a stick." I step over a large rock and remember how she lifted her arm into the air. "But it shimmered like a gold wand. And when she waved it, she vanished."

Becca giggles. "I'm sorry, Kelsey, but you can't seriously believe she had a magic wand. You've been reading too many fantasy books."

Leo's arched brows show he agrees with Becca. Maybe they're right and my imagination turned an ordinary stick into a wand. But that doesn't explain how the braided girl appeared and disappeared so quickly. I don't know what to think, so I shrug and hurry up the front steps with my friends. Becca hands me Trixie

Dad is waiting by the door, his expression like a forecast warning of stormy weather ahead.

"I'm taking Trixie upstairs," I say before Dad's thunder can crash down on me. "And I'll make sure she doesn't escape again. But she wouldn't have gotten outside if someone hadn't left the front door open," I add, so it's clear it wasn't entirely my fault. I gesture to my friends to follow. "Come on, I'll show you the room that's going to be mine. It's not like any room I've ever had before—wait until you see!"

"Not so fast." Dad stops me with his deep voice.

Swallowing hard, I slowly look up at him. "Um... what?"

"You kids wait right here." Dad turns abruptly and strides down the hall.

"Uh-oh." I exchange nervous looks with Becca and Leo.

Leo frowns, and Becca gives me a comforting smile.

A few minutes later, Dad returns. He's holding a covered plate and doesn't look angry. In fact, he's grinning. He lifts the lid, and I inhale the delicious aroma of cinnamon and sugar.

"Chip Nibblers fresh from the oven," Dad announces proudly as he offers us each a bite-size cookie. "I experimented with the recipe, so they're sweet and salty. Let me know what you think."

Trixie wiggles in my arms, sniffing. "Trixie wants one," I say with a laugh.

"For a troublemaker, she has good taste," Dad says wryly. "But I don't think carob and peanut butter chips are on her diet. Still it could be an interesting project—cookies for rabbits."

I plop a cookie into my mouth. Delicious sweetness melts on my tongue. Yum.

We thank Dad and hurry up the stairs. When I reach the second floor, Trixie has fallen asleep in my arms. Once she's nuzzled into her bed, I lead my friends down a long hall to a narrow door.

"There can't be a room behind that door." Leo purses his lips in puzzlement and swivels to point to a deep-set window. "The view would be obstructed if there were a room."

"We go up," I say as I open the door to reveal a narrow, winding staircase. "I can get there from the main staircase, but I prefer my secret shortcut. I could have had a suite on the second floor, but this small room is perfect for me." We spiral up thirteen steps to the third floor, and I push open the door of a circular room with more windows than walls.

There are no curtains or carpet, and peeling paint flecks the walls.

"A round room!" Becca spreads her arms and slowly spins in a circle. "Coolness!"

"Turrets like this were originally designed for military fortification," Leo says in his smarty-pants tone. It used to annoy me because I thought he was showing off, but I've learned he's just a little awkward and a lot smart.

"I love the view," I say with a proud sweep of my hands toward the windows. "The room looked disgusting when I first saw it—trash all over and gross mouse droppings. I swept and scrubbed so it's clean, but there's still a lot of work to do like painting and replacing that cracked window before I can move in."

I smile at my future room, imagining how it'll look with furniture. My bed will face the panorama of windows so when I wake up I'll see treetops and birds. My dresser will go on the right, and my bookshelves will cover the wall to the left. I'll place my wooden chest at the foot of my bed so it's easy to open the hidden drawer and reach my notebook of secrets—where I write down all the secrets I know about friends and family.

There's no furniture yet, but the curved window seat makes a good bench. "The view is amazing from here," I say.

Leo nods. "From this high vantage point you have a 260 degree view of your property, which could be useful for a spy."

"Exactly," I agree, pleased Leo understands. "And it's private enough to hold a CCSC meeting. Want to have one now?"

"Official meetings should be held in the Skunk Shack," Leo objects.

"An unofficial meeting then," I say, compromising. "I found a new mystery for the CCSC to solve."

"The mystery girl by the river?" Becca guesses, but I shake my head.

"She's mysterious, but this is about a ghost and a treasure." I grin. "I'm going to tell you a ghost story."

Leo takes a handkerchief from the leather satchel he always carries, spreads it across the wooden seat, and sits down beside me. Becca clears a spot on my other side.

"It was a shivery, stormy night when Caroline heard the death bells," I begin in a low spooky voice. I repeat the story that Aunt Philomena told this morning about the first Trixie, the bells, and the ghost. When I finish, Becca shivers. "Poor Caroline."

"If she ever existed," Leo says doubtfully.

"But if she did, the treasure might exist too," I say. "If I found it, I could help my parents. They used all their savings to buy this house, and it'll take even more to fix it up."

"A real treasure would be coolness." Becca's dark eyes shine a reflection of my own hopes. "But are you sure it's inside the house? Could it be buried outside?"

"I'm not sure of anything—except that I want to find the treasure." I gaze through the window at treetops reaching for the sky. "It has to be something amazing like gold or diamonds."

"Or nothing." Leo folds his arms across his T-shirt. "A story with no factual basis is not proof of a treasure."

"We'll find proof," I say with determination. "Leo, you're so clever at finding info online. Would you research the history of this house?"

"Well..." His arms drop to his sides. "I will, but only to prove that the story is a fabrication. I do *not* believe in ghosts."

"But the real question is, do they believe in us?"

Becca teases.

Leo scowls. "That's illogical."

"Just because we can't see them doesn't mean they can't see us." Becca gestures around the room and lowers her voice to an ominous whisper. "There could be a ghost here with us right now, listening to our conversation."

"A ghost spy!" I clap my hands. "We could use one in our club. Hey, ghost, if you're listening, want to be an associate member?"

"I second the nomination," Becca jokes.

"I object," Leo says so seriously that I try not to laugh.

"We're just kidding," Becca quickly assures Leo, patting him on the arm. "It would be cool if a ghost spy could tell us where the treasure is hidden, but we'll have to find out on our own. I'll check with my friends to see what they've heard about this house." Her title in the CCSC is Social Contact Operative, because she collects friends the way I collect secrets. If there are rumors about this house, she'll find them.

"And I'll keep searching here," I add with a gaze out the window to a panorama of outbuildings, an overgrown garden, trees, bushes, and the ever-rushing river. So many places to hide a treasure. Where will I start? If only there were a map.

"I almost forgot!" Becca suddenly jumps off the window seat and reaches into her shirt pocket. "In the craziness of chasing your bunny, I didn't read the text I got earlier."

I remember her surprise at the text. "Who sent it?"

"My cousin Danielle. Remember her?"

"Yeah." I nod. Danielle is a vet tech, and she gave us cat supplies to help care for our kittens after we found them in a dumpster.

Becca taps on her sparkly pink phone. "I rarely hear from Danielle because she's busy with college and work. I wonder what she wants...oh no!" Becca's mouth drops open as she stares at her phone. "They can't do that!"

"What?" Leo and I ask.

"Danielle's volunteering at the shelter today and says there are too many dogs and not enough cages." Becca's voice rises with alarm. "Dozens of shelter dogs will be killed if they aren't adopted by the end of the month!"

"Mom said it was full, but I didn't realize it was that bad," I say with a sick feeling. "A lot of the pugs we helped rescue still need homes—especially the older dogs."

"It's horrible." Becca twists her pink-striped black ponytail. "Danielle wants me to spread the word on social media, but everyone I know who might want a dog has already adopted one."

"Including my grandmother," I add thinking of Buggy, the cute squishy-faced pug that Gran Nola recently adopted.

"I'd take one if Mom would let me." Leo's shoulders slump. "But she says a cat and fish are enough."

"We have to do something!" I jump up, ready to race off to the shelter and rescue all those poor dogs. But I just stand there with no idea how to help.

"Danielle asked me to post photos of the dogs online." Becca glances at her phone. "But there are too many dogs for all of them to find homes in a small town like Sun Flower."

"The solution seems obvious," Leo says with a spread of his arms. "The shelter needs to advertise outside of Sun Flower."

"Easier said than done." Becca's leopard-print scarf slips down her shoulder. "Most people won't adopt a dog without seeing it first."

"Unless the dogs came to them," I say as an image

of a large blue van pops into my head. "Mom showed me a picture of a mobile pet van the shelter wants to buy. It could transport lots of animals to malls and events so people from out of town can adopt pets."

"Coolness!" Becca says with an enthusiastic nod. "They should so get one."

"The fact that they haven't yet indicates a problem." Leo taps his chin thoughtfully. "My guess would be that the cost of the van exceeds the available funds."

"If you mean it's too expensive, yeah." I sigh. "Mom said they were offered the van for half price—which is a great deal but still too much. The shelter needs more than ten thousand dollars. And another shelter wants to buy the van, so if they don't get the money soon, they'll lose it."

"We can have a fund-raiser to earn the money," Becca says as if this is as easy as snapping her fingers. She touches the shiny crescent necklace around her neck, the symbol of her friend group the Sparklers. "The Sparklers had a huge turnout for a fashion show fund-raiser. I'd design cute doggie outfits for a fashion show, but the shelter dogs have a live-or-die deadline of the end of the month."

"According to my calculations," Leo spouts off,

"that equals fourteen days, ten hours, and thirty-six minutes to save the dogs."

"We can do it—if we can think of a quick and easy fundraising idea," Becca says with a confident lift of her chin. She heads for the door. "I'll ask Mom for suggestions. She's always working with our sanctuary volunteers on some sort of fund-raiser."

"I'll talk to my mom too," I say. "I have to work around here today, but I can go tomorrow afternoon. Let's meet in the Skunk Shack to talk about a fund-raiser—and the treasure mystery."

Becca nods, but Leo shakes his head. A guilty look crosses his face. "I can't go."

"Why not?" I ask in surprise.

"I'll be with my dad," he says. "It's our Sunday together."

"I didn't think that was a thing anymore." Becca arches a brow. "Your father canceled the last three Sundays."

"He's been busy, and he said he was sorry." Leo glances away. "Besides, he has something important to tell me. He's taking me out to lunch then to a movie of my choice."

"That's great," I say, although I'm worried that

Leo's father will disappoint him again. Leo doesn't talk about his emotions, but I know he was hurt when his father didn't show up for their last father-son Sunday.

"So we'll meet at the Skunk Shack after school on Monday," Becca suggests. "That gives us lots of time to think of some great fundraising ideas."

But will our ideas be good enough to earn over ten thousand dollars in less than two weeks? I wonder as I lead my friends out of the turret room and down the twisty stairs. That's a lot of money to earn in a short amount of time.

I'm still worrying about the shelter dogs after my friends go home, so to distract myself I climb up the stairs to check on Trixie. She's sleeping like a little angel bunny in her cage until she hears me. Her eyes pop open, and her whiskery nose twitches. She hops around her cage like she wants out, and she's just too cute to ignore, so I reach inside for her.

She's soft and smells like the fresh straw from her cage. She wiggles like she wants down. But I glance over at the kitty bed and catch Honey eyeing the bunny. Can I trust Honey not to eat Trixie? I remember Becca's warning and tighten my grip.

"I'll let you hop around in the hall," I tell Trixie

as I carry her out of the room.

I gently set her down and she sits there for a moment, her ears twitching. Then she leaps forward and hop-hops to the staircase.

"Get back here!" I shout as she scampers down the stairs.

She pauses near the bottom of the stairs and looks up at me with her cute bunny eyes. She paws on the wooden step, as if she wants to play. I scoop her into my arms. "You are not sneaking outside again."

Back on the second floor, I start to put Trixie down when I see my cat padding toward us. She must have jumped through the pet door.

"Go back in the room, Honey," I call out.

But my cat pretends not to understand—the big faker—and keeps following me.

My hands are too full of soft bunny to take her back to my room. So I hold Trixie tightly and make a run for the door at the end of the hall. Ducking into the stairwell, I shut the door to keep Honey out. Now she'll give up and return to the room.

It's stuffy in here and smells sour like mildew. The only way to go is up, so I climb to the turret room.

Trixie wiggles in my arms. I don't know much

about bunnies, but Trixie seems unusually excited. Her floppy ears twitch. She sniffs like she's on the trail of something yummy. She probably smells Dad's cookies on my hands. I test her sniffer by moving across the room to the window seat to see if she'll follow me. Her nose twitches, and she turns around. Curiously, I watch her ears flop as she hops toward the closed door.

Except she veers to the right side of the door, which is the only part of the windowed room with a faded puke yellow wall that has dark stains and cracked plaster.

Again and again, she pushes against the wall as if it's a pet door that will swing open.

"Silly bunny," I say both amused and concerned. Did we inherit a dumb bunny? "Stop hitting the wall. That isn't a door."

Sighing, I realize she either doesn't understand or she's ignoring me. And she continues to nudge against the wall. I glance down to brush off dust from my jeans then look back up.

Trixie is gone.

- Chapter 4 -
Puzzling Prints

I kneel on the floor to look closely at the wall. It's stained with peeling paint and faint outlines that look like the ghosts of furniture that once backed up to the wall. Is there a trap door or hidden panel? I poke at the wall and plaster crumbles to the floor. Sneezing at the dust, I study the bunny marks on the floor.

"Trixie, where are you?" The empty room flings my words back at me.

Pressing my head against the wall, I hear a whisper of movement, like the soft sounds of bunny feet. "Trixie! You *are* in there. But how did you get behind a wall?"

The bunny couldn't have left the room since the door is closed. There has to be a button or lever that opens a hidden panel. I feel for an opening but find nothing. I move my hand down to a strip of decorative molding trim on the bottom. Squinting, I lean closer and see tiny smudges. At first glance they look like dirt, but up close they have a definite shape like a painted tattoo of four tiny ovals over an uneven circle.

"A bunny print!" I compare the painted print with the faded dust prints Trixie trailed on the floor. A perfect match.

But who made it and why? When I was little, I got a time-out for painting on my bedroom wall. My wall "art" was messy, and I dripped paint on the carpet. But this isn't a typical child's artwork. It's too perfect, as if painted by a skillful artist.

A clicking nose from behind the wall makes me jump. "Trixie!" I call. "Is that you?"

The reply is a thump. Trixie's cry for help?

I spread my hands flat and press hard against the wall, desperation rising. I haven't even had Trixie for a full day, and she's already escaped the house, been stalked by my cat, and is now trapped inside a wall. I have to get her out!

Analyze the facts, I remind myself. Trixie's prints lead to the wall so she's definitely in there. And if she can get inside, there must be a way to get her out.

As I continue to stare at the wall, I notice faint cracks in the plaster. A few of them stretch up and across in oddly straight lines. I trace one with my finger and feel a narrow crevice. It outlines a perfect square about the size of Leo's tablet. Placing my palm at the center of the square, I push—and the square swings in to reveal a hole.

"Trixie?" I call into the narrow opening.

All I can see is darkness, until sun streams in from the windows behind me and two bunny eyes glint in the dark.

"You clever bunny," I say, both amused and annoyed. "Come out right now."

It's no shock that Trixie ignores me. I press my face to the opening and can make out the vague bunny shape. I hear her, too, nibbling like she's eating. I want to reach inside to grab her but there could be spiders.

Or ghosts, I think uneasily.

But I can't leave her, so I prop the door open with my elbow and reach inside. I jerk back when something creepy brushes my skin. I look down at my hand. Yuck. Grimy cobwebs dangle from my fingers.

I wipe my hand on my jeans, then make another grab for Trixie. But she hops into the darkness. *Drats, I can't see her.* The wall hole isn't very deep, but it stretches into pitch-black shadows. I'll need a flashlight.

"Trixie, I'll be right back."

I hurry out of the room, firmly closing the door behind me. I race down the stairs and through the hall to my temporary room. I dodge around the beds and boxes to open the closet where I keep my spy pack. It's hidden behind a suitcase where my sisters won't find it.

I grab my spy pack—actually a green backpack—and also some bunny treats, then race back to the turret room.

I plop my spy pack on the floor and unzip it, then sort through my spy tools. I push aside a black knit cap, laser pointer, wire, graphite powder, and a chain. I take out my flash cap, magnifying glass, and plastic gloves. I quickly put on the gloves, which I think of as spider protectors, slip the flash cap over my head, and flick on the powering light beam.

Kneeling in front of the wall opening, I shine the beam inside.

Trixie twitches her nose at me and makes a clicking sound like a complaint. She turns away from the light and nibbles something on the floor. Eww, gross. Whatever she's eating will probably make her sick. I reach out with gloved hands and grab her. She squeals. She squirms. But I am the human and she is just a little bunny, so I win.

Trixie is *not* happy about being dragged out of her hiding place—until I offer her a handful of bunny pellets. While she nibbles contentedly, I glance at the door to make sure it's closed and she can't escape.

Turning back to the hole, I shine my light inside and see cobwebs and a few pellets that look exactly like Trixie's rabbit food. Did someone leave the pellets here for Trixie? Is that why she hopped inside the hole? But who created this hole and why? The door is hinged from the inside so it's practically invisible. Was something more than rabbit pellets hidden in here? And how did Trixie know to go inside?

So many questions! And the only one with the answers is nibbling bunny food.

Even with the flash cap, it's hard to see deep within the wall hole. But as my light sweeps back and forth, something glints from a far corner.

Treasure!

As I reach out with my gloved hand, I try not to think of spiders, rats, and other things that creep around in the dark. I feel along the floor...nothing except cobwebs. But what's that? I grasp something smooth and solid, and pull back.

Light from my flash cap shimmers on a slender metal object.

A key.

- Chapter 5 -
Key to Mystery

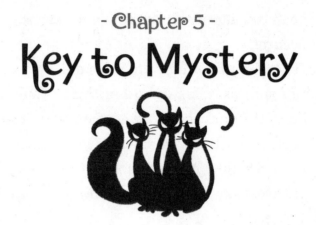

OMG! A key is almost as good as a map. Could it lead to an amazing treasure? Visions of gold coins and cash swirl in my head. I can't wait to tell my club mates!

If I had my own phone, I could send a text. But as the youngest in a family where money is tight, I'm out of luck. Sometimes when my sisters are in a good mood, they loan me their shared phone. But last time I saw them, they were scrubbing floors and griping about getting dirty—definitely *not* in a good mood. Besides, if I ask them or my parents for a phone, I'll get put to work immediately. And I'd rather work on this mystery first.

Tugging off my gloves, I put them back in my spy pack and sit cross-legged on the wooden floor. When Trixie hops over to curl up on my lap, I pet her soft, floppy ears and examine the gold key.

It's shaped like a skinny toothbrush, with a fancy loop on the top that's perfect for curling around my finger. It's old and rusty and wonderfully mysterious. I stare as if mesmerized as I swing it back and forth on my finger. How did it get inside the wall? How long has it been there? Does it lead to treasure?

The key is proof this house conceals a mystery — maybe several!

I've explored the house from basement to attic and didn't find any locked doors. Could the key unlock a hidden passage? Or maybe it opens a wall safe. In movies safes are hidden behind paintings or furniture.

But most of the furnishings were removed before we moved in. My hopes sink as I realize that this key could go to a piece of furniture that's no longer here. Only a few things were left behind — mostly junk, which was hauled away in a huge trash container. I won't give up looking until I find the right keyhole, even if it means searching every inch of this house.

Slipping my spy pack over my shoulders, I take Trixie to her cage, refill her water and food, then click the latch shut. "No more escaping." I wag my finger at her.

I head downstairs to start my keyhole search, when I hear Mom call my name.

"Kelsey, where have you been?" Her arms are crossed over a paint-splattered smock, her lips pressed in a disapproving frown. "You're supposed to be helping your sisters clean the walls."

"But I…" My excuses trail off and I feel trapped like a bunny in a cage. There's no escaping my chores—not even for treasure hunting.

Mom gives me a bucket of soapy water and a scrub brush, and I join my sisters in the living room. My brother—lucky guy—is working today at his pizza restaurant job. Kenya and Kiana wear old jeans and baggy T-shirts and matching expressions of disgust. With a sigh, I dip my brush into the pail of sudsy water.

"Did I mention I hate scrubbing walls?" Kiana complains. "Just look at my poor hands. My blisters have blisters."

"Like you're the only one? My hands are totally ruined." Kenya holds out her reddened hands, but I don't see any blisters. My sisters are such drama queens.

Kiana groans like she's being tortured. "After this I am so going to need a manicure."

As they make plans for a spa day, I'm only half listening. I gaze around the vast living room and imagine how grand it must have looked when Caroline lived here. What did the old lady call it? A parlor. I can almost see old-fashioned furniture and the twinkling lights of a chandelier shining prisms across the room. Ladies would dress formally in long skirts and dainty gloves. They'd have tea and polite (boring) conversations while a musician probably played a piano softly in the background. But they must have whispered secrets, too, and somewhere in this house is a hidden keyhole.

Could it be in this room?

The walls are bare except for jagged cracks and decades of grime. But the hidden panel in the turret room wasn't visible either, blending into the wall so invisibly that I might not have found it without Trixie. Could there be another hidden wall panel in here?

As I scrub the walls, I feel along the cracks and find...nothing.

A short while later, my father announces it's time for dinner. Even though the house is a chaotic work in progress, Dad insists that we follow family tradition and gather at the dining table for dinner. The only one missing is Kyle, who is still at work, as we sit in our usual spots around our formal dining table, amid moving boxes. Dad's creamy burrito casserole is delicious. I inhale the yummy aroma. So much better than smelling cleaners and paint.

Later that night, while my siblings are downstairs watching TV, I pull out my notebook of secrets. I haven't had a chance to tell Becca and Leo about my discoveries, so I write to myself.

> Secret 47. Trixie disappeared into a hidden panel in my turret room where I found an old gold key that may lead to a treasure.

I place the key under my pillow and fall asleep dreaming of secret passages. At first the dreams are fun as I discover mysterious passages and keyholes. I twist the key into keyhole after keyhole…but none of the doors open.

I wake up the next morning feeling frustrated.

My sisters are both still asleep and dawn is only winking, not quite awake.

I'm dying to tell my friends about the key and hidden passage. Leo will be hanging out with his Dad today, but Becca will be home. And she's usually up early to help her mother care for their menagerie of animals that includes a bear, a playful monkey, and a very scary alligator.

Tiptoeing across the room so I don't wake my sisters, I borrow their phone and quietly step out of the room and into the hall.

I send a quick text to Becca.

Found clue!

Cm ASAP

Immediately I get a reply from Becca.

Can't :(

Mucking stalls 2day

What clue????

I don't tell her. She'll have to wait to hear until tomorrow.

After returning the phone, I slip on my flash cap and set off to hunt for treasure.

I begin my search with the three spacious suites on this floor. Once they're remodeled, they'll belong to my sisters and brother until my siblings go off to college. Then the rooms will be turned into guest bedrooms for the B and B. My parents want to keep the original name of Down the Rabbit Hole and call the suites the Cheshire Cat, the Red Queen, and the Royal Tea Party.

I start in the suite Kyle chose for himself. It's empty, and the walls have some fist-sized holes like someone used them for a punching bag. I run my hands along each wall and peer into the holes but find nothing. So I move to the bathroom, which is missing a toilet and has a cracked mirror over the stained sink. I search the bathtub, shower, and cabinets. I'm running my hands down the sides of a bathroom cabinet when I feel something strange: a slight indentation. I press it, hoping it's a button. But my finger pokes right through the wood. Oops.

Sighing, I leave the room, hoping I'll have better luck in Kenya's chosen suite, when I hear Mom calling for me. Reluctantly, I give up my search and go downstairs.

Mom waits at the bottom of the staircase with a huge smile.

"We're having a party!" she announces so cheerfully that I almost believe she means this in a good way—until I notice the paintbrushes and cans.

So it is not the kind of party with balloons and cake, but a painting party. And it won't be over until the living room and kitchen are painted.

The key in my pocket calls to me, but I can't answer.

The next morning I'm so exhausted that I sleep through my alarm, and my sisters literally have to drag me out of bed. But after a quick breakfast, I'm wide-awake and have mysteries on my mind as I pedal to school.

Winding through Sun Flower reminds me of previous CCSC cases. A zorse named Zed ran into traffic on Pleasant Street, which led us to the alley where Becca, Leo, and I rescued three kittens from a dumpster. A few more turns and I pass a familiar yard full of golden sunflowers, where Sunflower Mary, a crafty old woman, rocks in her porch chair, yellow crochet yarn dangling down her skirt.

By the time I reach school, the warning bell is ringing.

I rush to homeroom to show Becca the key.

But she's busy talking to my worst-enemy-who-pretends-to-be-a-friend, Tyla. They both wear identical crescent moon necklaces like all Sparklers. I was a Sparkler for a while, but it didn't last long. The club is cool when they do community service, but not when Tyla bosses everyone around.

I don't get a chance to talk to Becca until class is over. I shout her name over the thundering herd of kids exiting the room. She doesn't hear me until I come up beside her and grab her arm.

"Becca," I whisper into her ear. "I found something exciting!"

"What?"

I notice model-tall, brown-eyed Tyla coming our way and shake my head. "We can't talk here. Tell you later," I say hastily.

"Lunch," Becca whispers back.

I nod, and we split up in different directions.

But at lunch, Becca is surrounded by Sparklers: Chloe, Sophia, and Tyla sit at their front-and-center table. I always sit with my sporty friends Ann Marie and Tori. We've known each other since kindergarten, when our parents called us the "Turbo Triplets." We were inseparable until my family lost our house to foreclosure and moved to an apartment. We grew apart not only because we weren't neighbors anymore, but also because Ann Marie and Tori are busy with sports. But we still eat lunch together.

As I head for my usual table, I glance around for Leo. He's not at the back table and neither is his friend (and CCSC associate member) Frankie. They're probably hanging out in the drama supply room again.

"Kelsey!"

I turn and see Becca waving me over to the Sparkler table. I want to show her the key but not in front of the others. The Sparklers dazzle the world in sunshine while I prefer to observe quietly from the shade. Becca, Chloe, and Sophia are all cool, but Tyla has a mean-girl streak wider than her fake smile. When she attacks me with subtle insults, Becca tells me to just ignore her. But it's not easy.

Becca is excitedly waving with both arms, so what else can I do?

Reluctantly, I go to the Sparkler table.

"Hey, Kelsey." Blue-haired Sophia glances up with a timid smile. Sophia recently starred in the school's production of *The Lion King,* so you'd think she was outgoing. But Sophia is surprisingly soft-spoken and shy.

"Want to sit with us?" Chloe looks up at me through big, jeweled glasses and makes room beside her.

I shake my head and gesture across the room. "I'm already sitting with some friends."

"The jocks," Tyla says with a demeaning roll of her dark eyes. "Don't they ever shower? I can smell them from over here."

I grind my teeth and narrow my eyes.

"Kelsey!" Becca grasps my arm. "Didn't you have something to tell me?"

I'd rather tell Tyla why she's the one who stinks, but I don't want to make things awkward for Becca. "Yeah," I say. "Let's go outside and talk."

"Can't you talk to her in front of us?" Tyla demands, standing tall so she towers over me. "Or is this a secret you don't trust us to hear?"

"Not a secret." Becca assures, her smile never faltering. "Kelsey and I are trying to help the animal shelter. Remember, I posted about all the poor dogs that might die if they aren't adopted soon?"

"Those poor dogs. It's so tragic." Sophia purses her dark-red lips, looking close to tears. "I begged my father to let me adopt another dog, but he said three was already too many."

Becca sighs. "That's the problem—there are just too many dogs and not enough people in Sun Flower to adopt them. That's why Kelsey and I want to help raise money so the shelter can buy a pet-mobile."

"I love fund-raisers!" Sophia says as she claps her hands. "What are you planning?"

"Um...that's what I was going to tell Kelsey." Becca hesitates. "I talked to my cousin Danielle who works at the shelter about a fund-raiser, and we decided to organize a dog wash because it's easy and they already have most of the supplies we'll need. She wants to have it this Saturday."

My mouth falls open. "So soon?"

"The dogs don't have much time," Becca reminds me. "We'll set up in front of the animal shelter, and while Danielle and other volunteers collect donations, we'll invite our friends to help wash dogs. It'll be fun."

"And messy," Tyla says with a flick of her glittery fingernails.

"Does that mean you won't help?" Becca asks.

"I'm all about helping." Tyla sits back down at

the table and touches her shimmering necklace. "Washing filthy dogs is a wonderful idea. It's so sweet how far you'll go to help the shelter—even washing smelly animals. And of course, I want to help too."

"You will?" I ask, surprised.

"Absolutely!" Tyla grins. "The other Sparklers will also volunteer."

"Great," I say, and I mean it. Even though Tyla isn't my favorite person, we'll need all the help we can get to wash lots of dogs.

"But we'll contribute with Sparkler style," Tyla adds with a lift of her chin. "Why get all wet and stinky by washing dogs when we can beautify them with makeovers? We'll give them a doggie spa treatment with painted toenails and sparkly ribbons. We'll earn lots of money for the shelter." She looks directly at me. "Way more than your dog wash."

"I doubt that," I say through gritted teeth. "People care more about a clean dog than frilly ribbons and nail polish."

"If that's a challenge, you'll lose," she says coolly.

I fake a smile. "I guess we'll find out."

Challenge accepted.

- Chapter 6 -
Changing Winds

After school when Becca and I meet at the bike rack, she doesn't smile, and her peach-frosted lips are pursed. Uh-oh. This is *not* good.

Bending over to unlock my bike, I glance uneasily at Becca. "Are you going to say anything?"

"You've already said too much." Becca spins the combination to her bike lock. "Why couldn't you ignore her?"

"You mean Tyla?" I ease my bike out of the rack.

"Who else?" Wind whips her ponytail across her face and she shoves it away. "This is about helping animals, but you and Tyla turned it into a competition."

"Don't blame me," I argue. "She's the one with the snotty attitude."

"You never give her a chance. She just wants to help."

"Her kind of help is poison. I don't know why you put up with her."

"She's my friend." Becca shoots me an icy look and grabs her bike's handlebars. I reach for my bike too.

Leo rolls up on his gyro-board. He grins at us. "Ready to go to the Skunk Shack?"

When neither Becca nor I say anything, he looks between us with a puzzled look. "We *are* having a meeting. Affirmative?"

"That's the plan." Becca gestures toward me. "Unless Kelsey doesn't want to go."

"I'm coming," I snap.

"Fine," Becca snaps back.

"I wouldn't miss our meeting for anything," I add coolly.

"Great," she says in a tone that doesn't sound great at all.

"Race you there!" Leo, being the most socially clueless person in the world, grins then zooms ahead on his robotic skateboard.

I don't know what to say to fix things with Becca, so I pedal after Leo. His skateboard is faster than our bikes and soon he's out of sight. The day started out sunny but clouds have rolled in and a wind kicks up, making pedaling uphill a struggle. Loose tendrils of my hair fling in my mouth and I spit them out. Becca's tires whirl behind me. Although she's close, it feels like we're miles apart. I know I'm right about Tyla, but maybe I'm wrong too, expecting Becca to choose between her friends.

As we reach the dense woods where the CCSC clubhouse is hidden high above the wild animal sanctuary, the wind whips stronger gusts. When I glance back, Becca is further behind. I open the gate and hold it wide for Becca. As she rolls through, our gazes meet. I think maybe she'll say something. Instead she whirls into thick bushes that seem to swallow her.

I latch the gate and hop back on my bike, hurrying on the bumpy trail. Leo's gyro-board leans against the cottage that once was used for sick animals. And sitting on the giant stump we sometimes use as a bench is Becca. I give her an uncertain look that asks, "Are we still friends?"

Instead of answering, Becca gestures for me to sit on the stump.

I prop my bike on its kickstand and hop up beside her. "Becca, I didn't mean what I said about Tyla."

"Yeah, you did...but it's okay." She clutches her ponytail so it doesn't fly with the gusting wind. "Sorry."

"I'm even more sorry." My shoulders sag. "I shouldn't let Tyrant Tyla get to me."

"She gets to me too," Becca admits. "But we've been friends for so long, her bossy attitude doesn't bother me much. Sometimes I even tell her no. Still, it's easier to do what she wants because she has good ideas. She's really fun when you get to know her."

I don't need her kind of fun, I think. But I don't say this to Becca.

We scoot off the stump and enter the clubhouse.

"So what's this big discovery of yours?" Becca shuts the door behind us. "I've been trying to guess all day. Did you find money or jewels?"

"Not this time." I think back to the discoveries we made not long ago in a tree house and shake my head. "What I found isn't worth much, but it could lead to a treasure. I brought it to show you and Leo."

"Let me see it already," she says impatiently, so I reach for my pocket.

"Wait!" Leo shouts so abruptly that I drop my hand. "Before you discuss club business, we need to officially call our meeting to order."

"What I found is too exciting to wait," I argue.

"My research has yielded interesting information as well." Leo slips into his chair at the stained table we use for club meetings. "We can all share our information and follow club procedure."

"I motion that we start our meeting," Becca says quickly.

"I second it." I slip into my lopsided chair. My chair wobbles as usual so I shift sideways.

"I hereby call this meeting of the Curious Cat Spy Club to order." Leo taps his pencil on the table, looking like a lawyer or judge in his button-down blue shirt and black vest. He's so organized that he's already set out our juice packets and chips on the table. I smile when I see he's chosen corn chips for me—my favorite.

I lift my hand. "I motion that we skip the usual boring reading of the minutes and treasury report and go straight to new business."

"Fine." Leo shrugs. "You may proceed."

"Look what I found!" I hold up the key like it's as precious as a hobbit ring.

"That's all?" Becca's leopard-print scarf sways as she shrugs. "What's exciting about a key?"

"That depends on what it unlocks," Leo says with a thoughtful look at me. "Do you know what it goes to?"

"No idea," I admit. "I was hoping you could help me find out."

Leo holds out his hand. "May I examine it?"

I drop the key into his flat palm. "It's metal like a skeleton key," he says, "but the bits haven't been filed down."

"I've never met a skeleton with a key," Becca jokes.

"Not a literal skeleton." Leo rolls his eyes. "A skeleton key is a master key with a serrated edge that's been filed down so it can open multiple locks. This key is rusty and heavy. It could be a century old."

"Wow!" I take the key back from Leo and swing it from the end of my finger like it's swaying to music. "Is it valuable?"

"I doubt it." Leo shakes his head. "Where did it come from?"

"I found it"—I pause because that's what detectives do in mysteries before they reveal an exciting clue—"in a hidden wall panel! And Trixie led me to it!"

"Your rabbit?" Leo's blond brows rise skeptically.

"Rabbits can be very intelligent," Becca says.

"You say that about all animals," Leo points out.

"Only because it's true."

"Trixie is really smart," I agree, then describe how the bunny disappeared into the hidden wall panel, leading me to the key.

"Only you don't know what the key goes to," Becca says when I finish.

"And it won't be easy to find out," I say with a sigh. "Most of the furniture was gone before we moved in, so the keyhole is probably gone too. I've checked all the doors, and it doesn't fit any of them."

"Maybe it fits something that's hidden behind a secret passage like the one you found," Becca says excitedly.

"Not a passage, just a hole. But there's one hidden panel, so there could be more. I'm going to find them," I add, dreams of treasure dancing in my head.

"And we'll help you," Becca says. "But we need to work on the fund-raiser first. Danielle will set up tables and supply buckets, towels, and dog shampoo. But it's up to us to get volunteers. I'm going to text everyone I know."

"I'll ask Ann Marie, Tori, and my family," I offer.

"I'll convey the information to Frankie, and he'll relay it to his drama club but—" Leo glances away guiltily. "I can't go."

I frown. "Why not?"

"I already made plans with Dad and Jessica."

"Jessica?" Becca and I repeat in surprise.

Leo taps his pencil nervously on the table, his cheeks reddening. "When Dad picked me up yesterday, he wasn't alone. He introduced me to his friend, Professor Jessica Chin. She teaches physics at the Socrates Academy for Gifted Children. We're going to Berkeley on Saturday so I can meet her daughter Riley."

"How old is Riley?" I ask uneasily.

"Eleven. But she's advanced for her age and taking college-prep courses at Socrates Academy."

I do *not* like the idea of Leo hanging out with a girl who is smart like him. Not that I'm jealous. That would just be childish.

Becca folds her arms. "Leo, this dog wash is important. We need all the help we can get to save the dogs. Can't you change your plans?"

"I don't know. But I'll ask my dad." Leo drops the pencil, and it rolls beside his unopened bag of chips.

With this settled, sort of, we switch back to club business, and Leo tells us what he's discovered about my house.

"It was built in 1927 and owned by Jacoby Whitney, who married Agnes Hampstead. They had only one child, a girl named—"

"Caroline Olivianne Whitney," I finish.

Leo nods.

"So Caroline was real, not just part of a ghost story," Becca says as she sips strawberry juice. "Did she really drown?"

"That's the official cause of her death, although her body was never recovered." Leo points to a copy of an old newspaper article with the headline "Birthday Girl Perishes in Raging River." There's a grainy black-and-white photo of a girl with dark ringlets wearing a ruffled dress and hugging a bunny with floppy ears; one white and one dark.

"The first Trixie," I murmur and scan the article that matches Philomena's story, except there's no mention of a ghost bunny or death bells, only the tragedy of a young girl who drowned on her birthday.

"Here's another printout with information," Leo adds, waving a paper at us. "The obituary for Jacoby Whitney, dated 1963. He died following a long illness, with no living heirs. He's described as a salesman who traveled frequently."

I sigh. "Nothing about searching for his daughter or a hidden treasure."

"Or ghosts," Becca teases.

"Logic and science disprove the existence of ghosts," Leo says like he's reciting from a textbook.

"Tell that to the ghosts," I say, not able to resist joking. I lower my voice to a spooky tone, "Beware the ghost bunny."

"Nothing scary about a cute bunny." Becca laughs.

"Trixie scared me when I thought she was lost outside," I admit. "But I won't let her escape again. I'll only let her out of her cage when I can watch her. If I follow her, she might even lead me to another hidden panel."

"You think there are more?" Becca leans closer, her dark eyes twinkling.

"I sure hope so! Philomena said Mr. Whitney had mysterious packages delivered to him. But nothing valuable was found after his death. So what was in the packages?"

"Good question." Leo taps his chin thoughtfully. "Since I've found evidence to back up some facts of the story, it's possible there was a treasure, too. We should investigate. I suggest we interrogate Philomena."

"Interrogate?" I can't help but giggle. "She's a nice old lady, not a criminal."

"But she may know what was in the packages," Leo says.

I shrug. "It can't hurt to ask her. She lives with our realtor, so Dad will know her address."

We hang out a while longer then clean up and head to our separate homes. Becca takes the dirt trail shortcut to her house while Leo and I ride down Wild Road. We split up as we reach downtown Sun Flower. He heads for his suburban home near Helen Corning Middle School, and I roll down Pleasant Street.

I'm thinking about secret panels as I wind through residential streets, and I almost pass the yard full of golden sunflowers without waving to

Sunflower Mary. It's magical the way sunflowers grow in her yard, even out of season. I got to know her after she helped the CCSC solve a mystery. She's rocking in a chair on her porch, and we wave to each other as I whirl by.

When I turn on the rustic road that leads to my new home, sounds quiet to a whooshing wind through trees and the rushing river. There are no cars or other bicyclists, which is a good thing, since the road is narrow and doesn't have a bicycle lane.

While my wheels spin, my mind travels decades into the past. I imagine Caroline as a child riding her bike to school on this very road. Was it paved back then? Or was it just a dirt trail winding along the river? What was it like to live here almost a century ago?

I slow at the faded sign that says Down the Rabbit Hole, Bed-and-Breakfast Inn and turn into the private driveway. My tires thump-thump across the wooden bridge. I slow my bike, swinging one leg over, ready to hop off. But I stop mid-hop when I catch movement across the yard.

At the edge of the property, where tangled berry bushes sweep down to the river, a figure stares up at my house.

The bright red braids and gold wand are unmistakable.

The magic girl!

- Chapter 7 -
Magic Girl

She's so focused on the house that she doesn't notice me.

The wand in her hand reflects the sun like it's on fire. And there's an intense expression of longing on her face. There are so many questions I want to ask her. What's she doing here? Where does she live? And why is she carrying a wand?

Abruptly, she turns toward me. I hold my breath, afraid she'll disappear if I move. All I can hear is my own thudding heartbeat, as if the world has hit a pause button. The sounds of the rushing river and blustering wind fade away. It's like she's cast a spell on me. And when her gaze locks with mine, I sense she has questions too.

But she whirls around and ducks behind a tree.

Gone again!

She's not getting away this time.

I drop my bike to the ground and take off running. She can't go far because the tree backs up to the prickly bushes tangling down to the river. If she tries to get through them, she'll get stabbed by thorns.

Yet when I look behind the tree, all I see is a wall of bushes.

Where did she go?

For a moment, I wonder if she simply waved her wand and transported to another place. Magic always seems so real when I read about it in my favorite books. I can imagine myself learning transfiguration at Hogwarts, shivering in a Narnia snowstorm, and traveling through time from a tree house.

Shaking crazy ideas out of my head, my gaze drops down to strange marks on the ground. Not footprints like I'd expect, but handprints.

Kneeling, I place my hands over prints that are slightly smaller than mine. The prints lead into the bushes. I push aside branches and peer into a dark hole. With a gasp, I realize I'm staring into a tunnel through the berry patch. Dropping to the ground, I crawl forward on my hands and knees, feeling like Alice plunging into the rabbit hole.

A hanging vine snags my hair. I push it away, trying not to think of spiders and snakes. The rushing sound grows louder, and I realize I'm headed down toward the river. As sun shines through vines, I can make out fences on each side of me. So this is how Magic Girl seemed to vanish! This isn't a tunnel—it's a fenced path. I suspect it was once a well-used trail to the river until berry vines and time swallowed it whole.

I step out on the riverbank, brush dirt and leaves from my jeans, then follow a well-worn trail over rocks, under trees, and around a curve. Finally, I reach a small clearing with a boat dock. Boulders block me from going further down the river, so I look around until I find the path again. It's rocky and I slip once but grab onto a bush. When I reach the top of a grassy hill, strange sounds float on the wind; sorrowful moans, screeching, and pounding drums blend in a chaotic harmony.

And down in a valley, I see a house.

It's rectangular with an attached garage and yellow with white trim. Flowers bloom below a large front window and wicker chairs on the wide wrap-around porch seem welcoming.

Someone grabs my arm.

I cry out and spin around to face Magic Girl.

Her red hoodie is a shade darker than her rope-like braids, and her jeans have rips in the knees. She holds her wand like a weapon, aimed at me. "Why are you following me?" she demands.

"Me?" I gasp. "Why were *you* sneaking around *my* house?"

"I wasn't..." She glances down at her grass-stained sneakers. "Not really."

"I saw you there twice." The strange sounds in the distance continue to shriek and moan, so I raise my voice as I stare her down. "I called after you, but you went through the bush tunnel."

"You found the tunnel?" Her shoulders sag, and she tucks her wand in her pocket. "I thought I was the only one who knew about it."

"Well, I know now. But I don't know why you were spying on my family."

"I wasn't spying on anyone."

"Then what were you doing at my house?"

"You only just moved in. I can go there if I want." Her voice rises with sharp, accusing edges. She's about my age, yet I've never seen her at school. I had no idea this house was even here. It is far off the road and tucked in a blanket of trees.

I fold my arms over my chest. "You were trespassing," I point out.

"I wasn't hurting anything. I just wanted to find my…" She purses her lips and stares down at her mud-splashed sneakers.

"Find what?" I demand.

She narrows her green eyes as if trying to decide if I'm an enemy or a friend. I'm wondering the same thing about her. When she finally opens her mouth, her reply is lost in a sudden clashing of horns, strings, and drums coming from the house. But I can lip-read, so I know her one-word answer.

"Prize?" I raise my voice to be heard. "What prize?"

She shakes her head, pursing her lips firmly.

My curiosity rises like the clashing chords of music. Her gaze shifts toward the house, as if she's afraid. I remember interrogation advice from my spy book, *Criminals and Crimes: Use a Suspect's Fears to Discover the Truth.*

"So don't tell me." I shrug like I don't care. "There are other ways to find out. I'll go knock on the door and ask someone there."

"No! Don't!" she cries, grabbing my arm.

"Why not?"

"Just go away." Her eyes flash fear while instruments from inside the house clash like warring musicians.

"I'm not leaving," I say as I lift my chin stubbornly, "until you tell me what's going on."

"Okay...but we can't talk out here in the open." She tugs on my arm, leading me around a driveway and behind the house. I duck beneath a hanging branch as we enter an orchard of fruit trees, some dormant like spring skeletons, but most blooming red, white, and pink blossoms.

"They won't see us here," she says with a furtive glance over her shoulder.

"Who are we hiding from?" I brush away a gnat.

"Them." She gestures toward the house.

The loud music softens and sweet voices rise in a harmony. "Does somebody have a band?"

"My whole family." She rolls her eyes. "Even me—although all I do is shake a tambourine. They joke that I can carry a tambourine but I can't carry a tune."

"That's harsh," I say sympathetically. My gaze drifts to the tip of the wand sticking up from her back pocket. "Does your family carry wands, too?"

"Wands?" She looks puzzled then slowly smiles. She reaches for her pocket. "You think this is a magic wand?"

"Well...um...isn't it?" I bite my lip and glance down at my sneakers. Maybe Becca was right and my imagination does get a little wild.

She tosses back her head and laughs. "I wish! I could use some magic," she adds as she holds up the not-a-wand.

"So what is it?"

"A retractable fishing pole." She holds it out. "See what happens when I press this button?"

The pole shoots up, stretching so it's almost as tall as I am. A reel unfolds and a hook dangles from the tip of the fishing line.

"Cool," I say, although to be honest I'm a little disappointed it's only a fishing pole.

The music from the house pounds with a drum solo that vibrates the ground. Seriously talented drummer. "Who's playing drums?"

"My oldest sister." She snaps the pole back to wand size and returns it to her pocket.

"What's the band called?" I ask.

She winces as if embarrassed. "Peanut Butter

and Jamboree."

I shake my head. "Never heard of them. But I'm not into country music."

"Me either." Turning, she goes over a low-hanging branch and grabs a cluster of bright red cherries. She offers me a few, and I plop one in my mouth. It's deliciously juicy, but she frowns like she bit into a sour cherry. "I am cursed with bad luck. I don't like country music, long road trips, or being a fake performer. I have zero musical talent. But my granny—she manages the band—insists that we all perform. So I bang a tambourine when we travel."

"Your family goes on tour?" I plop another cherry into my mouth. Hmm, even sweeter.

"Yeah, even my grandparents." She spits out a cherry pit. "Long, boring hours of being crammed into an RV. Grandpop does the driving."

She's frowning, but it sounds fun to me. "What about school?" I ask.

"Homeschooled." She shrugs. "Not that we're home much. And the motor home we travel in is so small, I sleep on an air mattress with my sisters. Not very glamorous. Mostly we perform at county fairs and festivals."

Now I know why I've never seen her at school.

One mystery solved, but many more to uncover.

"Traveling instead of being stuck in a classroom sounds exciting," I say.

"Not to me." She groans. "I'm the only untalented Holloway kid. Melody could sing at three years old, Sonata taught herself to play the drums, Jazzmine is a whiz with the guitar, and Reed plays the flute. Dad creates the costumes, Mom writes our songs, Grandpop drives the motor home, and Granny manages the business stuff."

"Wow! And I thought my family was big! Do you have a musical name, too?"

"Tragically." She sinks to the ground with an exaggerated groan. "Lyric."

"I like it." I push aside some leaves and sit cross-legged on the ground beside her. "I'm Kelsey. K names are the theme in my family. My twin sisters are Kenya and Kiana, and our older brother is Kyle. My siblings are okay...when they're not bossing me. Just because they're in high school and I'm in middle school, they don't take me seriously."

"I'm the youngest too." She twists a blade of grass between her fingers. "My family treats me like a cute pet. They feel sorry for me because the talent gene skipped me. I'd rather be bossed around than pitied."

"You wouldn't," I assure her. "Trust me on this."

She smiles. "Okay. I'll trust you."

"Enough to share your secret?" I ask hopefully.

Pushing her braids behind her shoulders, she sits up straighter to study me. "I'll tell you—if you help me."

I raise my brows. "Do what?"

"Get inside your house."

"Easy peasy," I say with a snap of my fingers. "Come over tomorrow after school. Well, after I get home from school. Tomorrow is a short day because of teacher meetings, so I'll be home by 12:30."

She nods. "Okay."

"Great!" I grin. "I'll invite my friends too. Leo and Becca will want to meet you."

"No!" Her voice rises, panicked. "Do *not* tell anyone about me."

My mouth drops open. "Why not?"

"If anyone finds out I have been sneaking to your place, I'll be in *big* trouble." Lyric glances uneasily toward her house where the singing and instruments have quieted. Even though we are too far away to be overheard, she drops her voice to a whisper. "I could be arrested."

I gasp. "Seriously?"

"Dead serious. You can't tell anyone you know me."

"But we're neighbors. Why shouldn't we hang out?"

"It's too risky." She grasps my arm a little too tightly, and I jerk back, suddenly uneasy.

What sort of trouble is she involved in? Is she a wanted criminal? Or maybe she witnessed a crime, and her family is in the witness protection program. But if they're hiding out, why form a band and give public concerts?

I stare at Lyric suspiciously. She looks like a heroine from my childhood novels, with cute Pippi-Longstocking braids and Anne of Green Gables freckles, but what if she's more villain than heroine?

"I should really go home." I step away from her, my foot crunching a brittle stick with a sharp crack.

"Please, don't!"

"Will you tell me what's going on?"

She sucks in a deep breath then blows it out. "You must promise not to tell anyone you know me."

I bite my lip, not wanting to make a promise to

someone I just met. But it's the only way to find out her secret. And I already have a notebook full of secrets. One more won't matter.

So I promise.

"About two years ago," Lyric begins, pausing to spit out a cherry pit into the high grass, "I was fishing on the riverbank near your house and caught a super gigantic fish." She stretches her arms wide. "I struggled to hold onto my pole, but the fish was too strong. It dragged me into the water and broke my pole. I'm not usually a crybaby, but I was wet and shivering and the fishing pole had been a birthday gift from my granny. I was so busy crying, I didn't know anyone else was there, until someone touched my shoulder. A fancy lady in a large yellow hat smiled at me. I'd seen her at church and knew she owned the big house by the river."

"Our realtor said the previous owner was a widow," I remember.

"Yeah. Mrs. Galano closed the B and B after her husband died." Lyric's red braid bobs as she nods. "I was cold and shivering, so she invited me into her house. She offered me a towel and hot chocolate with marshmallows and told her husband's fishing stories. She even gave me a retractable fishing pole that belonged to him." Lyric reaches around to her back pocket and fondly touches the shiny pole. "Meeting her was the luckiest thing that ever happened to me. When I'd go fishing, she'd visit me. The trail wasn't covered in berry bushes back then and was easy for her to walk through, even when she started using a cane. Sometimes she'd invite me inside for hot chocolate and to play with her bunny."

"Trixie?" I guess.

"I love that darling bunny." She smiles. "I'm glad she's living with you now."

"She's really cute, but she's an escape artist. When I first saw you, my friends and I were trying to get her back in the house."

"Tricky Trixie," Lyric says fondly. "I miss playing with her."

"Is that why you want to come over?"

"No." She shakes her head. "I want to look for treasure."

My eyes pop wide. "What do you know about the treasure?"

"Not *that* treasure. Mrs. G didn't believe in those rumors any more than she believed her house was haunted. I've been there lots of times and never saw any ghosts." She twists a cherry stem into a knot. "All the crazy rumors gave Mrs. G the idea for the treasure hunt game. She'd give me clues leading to a prize—usually a small gift like a hair tie or fishing lure." She smiles sadly. "But that day, while I was searching for the prize, she felt dizzy and said we'd have to finish the game tomorrow. Only she..." Lyric's eyes glisten with tears. "She died."

"How terrible." I want to reach out to hug her, but she's all stony like her skin is a hard shell holding her emotions.

"Bad stuff happens." She tosses the knotted stem away. "I forgot all about the game until a few weeks later when I dreamed of Mrs. G. She was so real, it was like she was in my room. She told me to go to the house and find the prize. But the house was up for sale and locked. Still, I had to try, so I climbed through a window with a broken latch. I was searching the kitchen cupboard when I heard strange noises. I freaked and ran outside—right into the sheriff."

My jaw drops. "Sheriff Fischer caught you?"

She nods, groaning. "I have the worst luck ever! Who knew there was an alarm system?"

"What happened?" I ask breathlessly.

"The sheriff threatened to arrest me if I tried to break into the house again. When he drove me home, my parents overreacted, like they always do. Their daughter, a law-breaker? Not acceptable! My family is wholesome and perfect." Lyric's freckles scrunch together as she scowls. "I was grounded for a month and forbidden to go back to the house. I gave up looking for my prize—until your family bought the house."

I stare at her, puzzled. "There's no way it's still there. When we moved in, there was only trash and some old furniture, most of it junk that my parents tossed out. Why search now?"

"Because Trixie is back." Her green eyes shine excitedly as she pulls out a small blue note from her pocket. "Here's the last clue Mrs. G gave me."

I read the handwritten words:

Follow the bunny.

- Chapter 8 -
The Bunny's Clue

Before I can ask her anything else, someone shouts, "*Lyric!* Come practice!"

Lyric scowls toward the house, where an elderly woman stands on the porch. She has a crown of silvery-red hair, and her flowery white skirt billows in the wind. Even from this distance, I can see her resemblance to Lyric.

"My granny. I better go bang my tambourine." Lyric's tone is pained as she shoves the blue note back into her pocket. "We'll talk more tomorrow."

"One o'clock," I say, nodding. "By the hidden trail."

"I'll be there." She waves and hurries off to join the band.

Chewing my last cherry, I turn around and head home. The rushing rhythm of the river drowns out Peanut Butter and Jamboree's music, and I puzzle over what Lyric told me.

Follow the bunny.

I already did that, and Trixie led me to the wall panel where I found the key. Could the key be Lyric's treasure? It's not much of a gift—unless it opens something amazing like a treasure chest. If I show it to Lyric, will she know what it goes to?

Rocks in the river path lie scattered like an obstacle course. I slip on a round rock and it rolls. Stumbling, I throw my arms out for balance. I step more carefully on a rock along the riverbank. I'll have to step carefully with Lyric too, I think as I continue along the path. While her story sounds logical, I have a feeling it's not the whole truth. What isn't she telling me? I sort through the sequence of events.

Mrs. Galano told Lyric to "follow the bunny" to find a treasure.

Sadly, the old lady died and the house went up for sale.

The bunny was cared for by our realtor.

Lyric tried to search the house and was caught by the sheriff.

If she hadn't been caught, would she have found the prize? It doesn't seem possible since the house had been emptied. Anything hidden there would also be gone—unless it was inside a wall. Could there be more secret panels?

I can't wait to tell Becca and Leo...only I can't. "Drats," I mutter, remembering my promise not to tell anyone about Lyric.

Prickly vines grab at me as I crawl through the berry-shrouded trail. I'm sweating when I come out. Brushing off dirt from my jeans, I'm surprised to see only Dad's SUV in the driveway and not Mom's animal control truck. She must be working late.

When I enter the foyer, there's a lingering smell of paint. I peek into the living room at the walls, which now shimmer a bright shade of Mellow Yellow Summer. Crystals glitter from the "great deal!" chandelier my mother found at a second-hand store. The room is arranged with antique-style wood chairs, a brocade couch, Dad's favorite leather recliner, and a cushioned window seat beneath an arched window where sunshine streams inside. Our house is starting to feel like a home.

But where is everyone?

I listen for sounds. Nothing. I start up the stairs but stop when I hear a thud from the kitchen! Is it Honey? Or did Tricky Trixie escape again? I detour into the kitchen and find Dad perched on top of the refrigerator.

I peer up at yellow paint-stained jeans. "Dad, why aren't you using a ladder?"

"A ladder would be an excellent idea." He twists to glance down at me. "Except it would take too long to find in that jumbled mess in the garage. Climbing is quicker." He reaches into a high maple-wood cabinet. "It has to be here somewhere..."

"What are you looking for?" I ask with an amused smile, guessing Dad is preparing another scrumptious dinner. When it comes to cooking, Dad is such a perfectionist. I teasingly call him a "food diva."

"Rigatoni pasta." Dad bangs the cabinet shut and opens the next one. "I'm positive I bought a package. But it's not here."

"Maybe it's still packed." I gesture to stacked boxes by the fridge.

Dad groans. "You're probably right."

"I'll help you look," I offer.

"Thanks, but it would be quicker to go to the

grocery store." Dad shuts the cupboard. "I need a few other things anyway."

"Wait, Dad," I say, thinking back to the CCSC meeting earlier today. "There's something I want to ask you."

"Sure thing, Kels." Dad jumps down with a thump and smooths back his dark hair. "What?"

"I want to visit our realtor's Aunt Philomena," I say. "To find out more about the ghost story she told us."

Dad grins. "She's quite a storyteller. But I hope you realize she was just entertaining you kids. Our house isn't haunted."

"Oh, I know that," I say, hoping there aren't any ghosts listening and laughing at me. "I'm curious about the history of our house. Philomena was here when she was young and probably knows a lot about the people who lived here. It would make, um, a good history report for school. Would you ask Mr. Dansbury if I can visit?"

"Elderly ladies love company," Dad says with an approving smile. "His house is on the way to the grocery store. If he's not busy, we can stop by. I'll call him right now."

I jump up to give Dad a hug. "Thanks!"

A short while later Dad pulls up in front of a spacious two-story home with a stained-glass front door and fancy wrought-iron railings on the balconies. Red and white rocks border planters blooming with yellow roses. Parked in the circular driveway is a sleek black sedan with the Dansbury Realty logo on the side.

A wheelchair ramp parallels the staircase leading into the house, and a middle-aged woman wearing a plaid scarf opens the door. "Nice to see you again, Mr. Case."

"Nice to see you too, Sally. I'm only here to drop off my daughter."

I give Dad a startled look. "You're not staying?"

"You're the one with questions, Kelsey." He musses my hair. "I'll only be at the grocery store for a half an hour."

The woman holds out her hand to me. "Hi, Kelsey. I'm Philomena's nurse," she adds. "I hear you appreciate a good ghost story."

I glance back as Dad waves. He climbs into his car and drives away.

"Come inside, but keep your voice down." Sally touches her finger to her lips. "Mr. Dansbury is busy in his office on a conference call."

I nod and follow Sally down the hall.

"Ah, here we are," Sally says. "Luckily, Philomena is having one of her good days. Still, if she falls asleep, wait a few minutes. She usually wakes right up."

Sally leads me into a spacious room, cozy with comfortable couches, chairs, and sunny windows. Philomena sits on a couch, with her wheelchair parked nearby, as she peers through her thick glasses at a paper on a low table. I look closer. She's muttering to herself as she does a crossword puzzle.

She doesn't seem to notice I'm in the room, and I stand there awkwardly. I wish I'd waited to come here with Becca and Leo. What if I don't know what to say? I'm used to talking with my grandmother, but Gran Nola is really active and into yoga and bicycling marathons. Philomena seems so frail, like if I sneeze she might fall over.

I'm still waiting for her to notice me when she blurts out, "What's a twelve-letter word for a German bell-playing instrument?"

"I don't know." The only German words I know are dog commands like *steh* and *platz*.

She waves my words away like pesky gnats. "I was speaking out loud, not asking for help. I will get this. I always do, it just takes longer for my memory to shift and to...*glockenspiel!*" She gives a triumphant whoop then waves the paper in the air. "Success."

She looks over and focuses on me. "Are you here for another ghost story?"

"No...um...not exactly." I shake my head. "I thought you could tell me...if you want...about Caroline's father."

"Not much to tell. I only met him once, and don't know much more than rumors." She sets down her pencil. Her shoulders are hunched, but her eyes are sharp. "But I do know why you're here."

I shift awkwardly on the carpet. "You do?"

"You can't fool me, young miss. You're after the treasure."

"Um...well...I am curious."

"Knew it." Her grin is smug, as if she can read my mind.

I sit beside her on the couch. "Was there really a treasure?"

"Naturally, people gossiped about Mr. Whitney, especially when he received packages labeled 'fragile' from faraway countries. The postmaster asked him about the packages, but his answer was always the same: 'Treasures.' A strange reply for an even stranger man." She clicks her tongue disapprovingly. "Rumors went wild, especially after he died and nothing valuable was found."

"How do you know?" I ask, mesmerized by her words.

"Because my nephew was one of the treasure hunters." She gestures toward her nephew's office. The door is open a crack, and I hear the low murmur of the real estate agent's voice. "When Dennis was young, his buddies dared him to spend a night there. That was before the house became a B and B, and it had a reputation for being haunted." She leans close, her eyes widening. "It was a long time ago, and a shivery, stormy night."

I try not to smile—her last story began with a shivery, stormy night too.

"Dennis told his parents he was staying the night with his friends. But he went to the deserted house. Alone. He climbed in a broken window. His buddies warned him about a ghost, but he wasn't scared. He was after the treasure. He'd only searched a few rooms when—" Her voice cracks, and she pauses to sip from a water glass.

"What?" I lean forward.

"As darkness settled on the house like a concealing cloak, Dennis heard strange sounds. Unearthly thumps, chimes, and footsteps."

"His friends could have been messing with him," I guess.

"That's what he thought too until..." Her words dangle like a hook on a fishing line.

I dig my fingers into the edge of the couch. "Until what?"

"He saw the ghost."

"A real ghost?" A ball of fear tightens in my stomach. *It's just a story*, I remind myself. Even if it happened, it was a long time ago, before I moved into the house.

"A strange ghostly shape floated over the staircase." She shivers. "Dennis described it as half animal and half human with glowing eyes and long ears. When it came after Dennis, he tried to run away but tripped and blacked out."

My hands fly to my mouth. "What happened next?"

She glances slyly at her nephew's office and lowers her voice. "He doesn't like me talking about the past."

"I won't say anything to him," I assure her.

"He woke up the next morning outside, lying by the riverbank. His shirt was ripped and his arms were scratched like he'd been clawed by a wild beast. When he got home, he was so terrified that he swore he'd never stay another night in that house."

"But he came back to sell the house to us," I point out.

"He always leaves before dark," she says. "Nighttime is fright time."

My heart quickens, but I hide my fears. "Do you really think my house is haunted?"

"I believe my nephew," she says without a doubt. "Both Caroline and her father died there. Tragedy sinks into the wood of a house and changes it forever."

I know she's trying to scare me. But I didn't come here for ghost stories; I came for the truth.

"My friends and I researched the house," I say purposefully. "We found an article about Caroline's death and her father's obituary, but nothing about treasure."

"He was very secretive about those packages he received with postmarks from foreign countries. I know the postmaster, and she told me the packages were marked fragile and insured as if very valuable.

But even though my nephew hired a cleaning crew and searched from basement to attic before it was sold, nothing valuable was ever found." She sips her water then stares deeply into my eyes. "There's one way to find the treasure—if you're brave enough."

I gulp. "How?"

"Wait for a rainy night and ask the ghost." She cackles just like a witch in a fairy tale. "Of course, no one has found a treasure, so either it's long gone or it was all just rumors."

"Unless it's hidden in the walls," I can't resist saying.

She leans forward eagerly. "Why do you say that? Did you find something?"

"Nothing really...just a small hole in the wall." I don't mention the key zipped in a pocket of my spy pack.

"The hole should be repaired. My nephew can recommend a repair service," she says.

"It's not a damaged wall," I assure her quickly. "Just a rabbit-sized cupboard inside a wall. I think Trixie played there a lot since there was still some rabbit kibble inside."

"Oh, sweet, curious Trixie," she says with a fond smile. "Whenever I let her out of her hutch, she'd hop up and down the stairs. I loved watching her. And she looks exactly like the first Trixie."

"Really?" I perk with interest.

"Same brown and white markings on her floppy ears. See for yourself. Caroline is holding her in the party photograph." She gestures to a display cabinet.

I cross the room to the wooden cabinet, which has four shelves. The top three display black-and-white photographs in antique frames, shades of gray from long ago. A silver-framed photo shows a group of girls in ruffles and bows surrounding a small pale-haired girl seated behind a two-tiered birthday cake. The birthday girl is blowing out candles, and a whiskery rabbit face peeks out from her lap. The first Trixie!

"It's the only photo I have of the party," the old lady says sadly.

My gaze drops to the bottom shelf, and I stare in surprise at a floppy-eared toy bunny made of a worn fabric. Around its neck is a collar of glassy red beads. "Is this the toy bunny from Caroline's party?"

"Yes. I carried it everywhere as a child. It's ragged now, but I can't bear to throw it out, so I keep it in that cabinet."

"The collar is so pretty. Are the beads real rubies?"

She shakes her silver-haired head. "Just painted glass. Of course, Caroline's toy bunny had a genuine ruby collar just like her pet Trixie. My toy bunny isn't worth much—except to me."

I look back up at the photograph. I scan the faces, trying to guess which one is Philomena. But I can't.

"I'm the girl on the end with the short bobbed hair," Philomena says, once more seeming to read my mind. In the photo, she stands off to the side with a shy smile, like she doesn't quite fit in with the other girls. I know how that feels.

"I never could grow my hair long like Caroline and her closest chum, Marjorie Ann," she adds wistfully. "Marjorie Ann is the tall girl in the middle with her arm around Caroline."

Something about Marjorie Ann draws me in. I can't stop staring. Her chin is lifted with determination and her confident smile gives me a familiar feeling, like we've met before.

But how can that be possible?

The photo was taken over eighty years ago.

I'm still puzzling over the strange familiarity of Marjorie Ann when I return home.

Doing the math, if Marjorie Ann is still alive, she's the same age as Philomena. She will be in her nineties. Wrinkles and time will have changed her drastically. So why does the tall, long-haired girl look so familiar?

Dad retreats into the kitchen where Mom sits at the table, writing in a notebook. There's giggling from the living room, and I peek inside. My sisters are watching a video on the phone they share. Whatever they're watching must be really funny. I start to join them until I remember that I need to check on my cat and bunny.

Hurrying up the stairs, I step into my room...and gasp.

The bunny cage is empty!

I start to panic until I see Trixie curled in my cat's plush kitty bed. How did she get out of her cage? She's a very naughty bunny, but I'm just relieved she's safe.

She looks so sweet in Honey's bed that I can't help but smile—until I see Honey crouched on a shelf over the sleeping bunny.

And Honey pounces.

Chapter 9

Leo's Surprise

"*Honey, no!* Don't eat the bunny!"

I race across the room, but I trip over a box. When I pick myself up, my cat is on top of the bunny. Her sharp-toothed mouth opens and...

Honey licks Trixie's furry face. Instead of munching on a bunny snack, my cat and bunny nuzzle together like best friends. And Honey purrs.

"Becca was wrong," I tell Honey, kneeling beside the kitty bed. I tickle her under her chin where she likes it best. "Some cats might attack a bunny, but not you."

Purring louder, my sweet kitty snuggles around the bunny. Trixie blinks at Honey, then closes her chocolate eyes and goes to sleep.

I smile at my two pets, and my heartbeat slows back to normal.

But how did Trixie get out of her cage? The cage door hangs open, but I know I shut it after I fed Trixie this morning. I check the latch, and it's not broken. Did someone unlatch it after I left for school? One of my sisters? Or is there a more ghostly explanation?

I glance across beds and boxes, searching for any evidence that I'm not alone. But there's no spooky chill or unearthly moans. And if there really was a ghost, my animals wouldn't sleep so peacefully. The only thing I sense is a stinky litter box. Sighing, I clean the kitty litter, replace the soiled straw in the rabbit's cage, and refill their water and food dishes.

Afterward, I follow the scent of savory meat sauce and tomato downstairs. Silverware clatters as Mom sets the table, and I spy Dad by the stove, stirring a large pot. In the living room, my brother is laughing along with my sisters. It's nice to have my family together. The only one missing is our dog, Handsome—the most gorgeous golden retriever and whippet mix. He's still at Gran Nola's house, but he'll join us when Dad repairs the backyard fence.

After moving from a large house to a small

apartment to a cottage to then being homeless, we finally have a forever home. My parents still have some money problems, and the house needs a lot of repairs, but it's our home now. And I'll do whatever I can to keep it that way—even if it means confronting a ghost.

As I'm pouring milk over my cereal the next morning, the phone rings. Leo asks me to stop by his house on the way to school for a CCSC meeting.

"Didn't you say meetings could only be held at the Skunk Shack?" I can't resist teasing.

"This is an official before-school meeting at an alternative location," he explains. "My mother will have croissants and beverages for us. I have something amazing to show you."

I wonder what it could be as I coast my bike up Leo's driveway. Although I've visited many times, I'm always awed by the stark whiteness of his house. Even the lacy window curtains are white. Leo's mother is obsessed with cleanliness, and she squirts my hands with a sanitizer before gesturing for me to go down the hall.

I follow the savory smell of bacon to Leo's room, which is high-tech. He has multiple computers, printers, and shelves of robotic inventions and labeled containers of tools and materials.

There's a tray with a pitcher of orange juice and plates of fresh fruit and golden croissants. Becca is already there, munching on a croissant. Leo's calico kitten sits on her lap, mewing hopefully at Becca's bacon and cheese croissant.

"Hi Leo, Becca, and Lucky." I pet the cute kitten we rescued several months ago from a dumpster.

"You're four minutes late." Leo taps the digital clock on his phone.

"It's good I made it at all." I toss my backpack on the ground and sink into a chair beside Becca. "I had to rush to get here and forgot to take a sack lunch."

"We won't need lunch after this amazing breakfast Leo's mom prepared." Becca gestures to her plate.

"So what's the exciting something you want to show us?" I pour a glass of orange juice.

"Look what my father gave me!" Leo gestures to a cluster of tiny tubes that look like weird spaghetti. "When Dad said he had a gift, I expected another T-shirt. But this is beyond my expectations."

"What is it?" I ask, reaching for a croissant.

"The cutting edge of biomimicry for building robotics."

I pause mid-bite to stare at him. "Um...bio-what?"

Leo gives me a "don't you know anything?" look. "Instead of building robots with heavy motors and servos, biomimicry uses multifilament muscles."

Becca sneaks a piece of bacon to Lucky, looking curiously at Leo. "I didn't know your father was interested in robotics."

"Dad isn't, but Professor Chin encouraged him to stimulate my intellectual curiosity. Her daughter, Riley, belongs to an advanced robotics club, and they have access to tech like this." He holds the spaghetti-like stuff with the same care of a mother cradling a new baby.

Becca smiles. "Coolness."

Freaky-looking stuff, but it's great to see Leo so happy. I'm glad his father is spending more time with him. But I'd rather Leo didn't hang out with the professor's clever daughter. Aside from being super smart, Riley is probably taller than me too.

After putting his gift away, Leo suggests having an official CCSC meeting. He starts with a treasurer's report ($54.14) then reads the minutes from the last meeting (I try not to yawn). Becca jumps in with news that the dog-washing fund-raiser now has an official name: Wag and Wash.

"I wanted to call it the Laundro-Mutt," Becca says, patting the kitten in her lap. "But Danielle already made the flyers and is passing them out."

"I'll be able to attend after all," Leo adds. "Dad changed the campus tour with Professor Chin and Riley to Friday after school. He's getting off work early so he can take me."

"I'm glad." Our eyes meet and I blush. "I mean, we need all the volunteers we can get. I talked to Tori and Anne Marie, and they have swim practice that morning but will come afterward to help."

"I've texted my friends." Becca licks crumbs off her fingers then counts off. "Trevor, Vince, Jenn, Alma, and Quinton are for-sures. Mom says she'll help, and she's going to ask our animal sanctuary helpers too."

"I proposed the project to Frankie." Leo pauses to wipe juice from his lips with a napkin. "He'll be there with members of his drama club."

"This fund-raiser is off to a great start!" Becca's dark eyes shine. "With that many volunteers, we can wash lots of dogs. And Danielle will supply hoses, buckets, and towels." She grabs her backpack. "We should hurry to school. I need to stop by my locker."

"Wait." I lift my hand. "I didn't tell you my news. Guess where I went last night?"

"The odds of us guessing are considerably low, unless you supply us with additional information," Leo says.

"Or just tell us." Becca pushes her giraffe-spotted headband away from her curious brown eyes. "Where were you?"

"Visiting Philomena," I say dramatically. "I asked her questions about my house, and she told me a ghost story about her nephew."

"The nervous bald guy who sold you your house?" Becca asks.

"Yeah." I switch to a creepy voice. "When Mr. Dansbury was a teen, his buddies dared him to search for treasure in my house. But a ghost shaped like a giant bunny chased him out."

"No way!" Becca's gasp startles Lucky, who jumps off her lap.

"Illogical and impossible," Leo scoffs.

I shrug. "Spooky stories are fun. He probably did accept a dare to sleep in my house, but I don't think a ghost *really* chased him. I'd have to be crazy to believe in a floppy-eared monster ghost."

"A giant ghost bunny?" Becca teases.

"Oooh, scary...not." I giggle.

Leo leans forward in his chair "Did you ask about Caroline's father?"

"Yeah, only she didn't know much. But she showed me the stuffed bunny she got as a party prize and an old photo from Caroline's birthday party." I sip my orange juice. "Caroline's best friend, Marjorie Ann, looks familiar. But that's crazy because she'd be really old now."

"Maybe she's the grandmother of someone you know from school," Becca suggests. "Mom often says I look like my grandmother. So Marjorie Ann's granddaughter might look like her too."

"Yeah, that's probably it," I say, relieved to have a logical explanation. "Philomena's stories may be exaggerated, but my spy book *Suspect Traits and Tells* says to 'Find the truth that lurks in every lie.' If there's a treasure hidden in my house, I'll track it down. I already have that old key. I'll bet something precious it opens a secret panel."

"That's an interesting theory but unlikely." Leo's tone is skeptical. "Statistically speaking, the odds of finding a nearly century-old treasure are astronomical."

"It'll be so fun to look," Becca says excitedly. "I wish we could skip school and start looking now."

"A treasure hunt party would be fun," I say. "All we have to do is follow the bunny."

Leo gives me an odd look. "Why would we do that?"

"Because that's the clue she—" I slap my hand over my mouth, remembering my promise not to tell anyone about Lyric.

"She?" Becca repeats. "Who?"

I feel my face reddening. Why did I agree to that stupid promise?

"I mean...um...Trixie," I say quickly. "She led me to the key, so maybe she'll lead us to other hidden panels."

"It would be a futile effort to follow an *Oryctolagus* around," Leo says.

"I guess that's some fancy word for rabbit." I roll my eyes.

"Latin," Leo answers. "I'll bring my scanner so we can search for a hidden passage scientifically with radar technology that can detect something hidden behind a wall. By studying radio waves, I can identify any objects on the other side of a wall."

"Coolness!" Becca finishes drinking her orange juice and jumps from her chair. "Let's do some high-tech treasure hunting at Kelsey's house after school. If we find the treasure, we can buy the mobile pet van for the shelter. Think of all the animal lives we can save!"

I wish I could say, "Great plan, let's do it!" But I already made plans to meet with Lyric for a different treasure hunt. I want to help her follow her clue, but I also want to search for a hidden passage with my club mates.

How can I do both?

My shoulders slump as I force out the words. "We can't search today."

"Seriously?" Becca plants her hands on her hips. "Why not?"

"I'm already busy...um...I have to do something at home."

"That's not a problem. We can help with your chores," she offers. "You've helped me lots at the sanctuary, cleaning up stalls and feeding the animals."

"It's nothing like that." I blow out a heavy breath. "I'm meeting someone."

Leo gives me a startled look. "Who?"

"You don't know her…" Drats! My friends are looking at me like I'm a suspect of a crime. I don't want to lie, but I can't tell them the truth and…

A ringing phone saves me.

Leo reaches over for his cell on his desk. When he glances at the screen, a strange expression—something like embarrassment—crosses his face. "It's Dad."

"Tell him hi from us," Becca says cheerfully.

Leo doesn't answer. His strange expression gets stranger. He shakes his head and crosses to the other side of the room where he speaks too softly for us to hear.

"What's up with him?" Becca whispers, frowning. "Why is he being secretive about a call from his father?"

"Very odd," I say, relieved that the target of suspicion has shifted from me to Leo. So I do what any amateur spy would do and read his lips.

"…Friday decide if you…tour the campus." Leo smiles at something his father says.

What campus? I wonder. And then I remember that his father's professor friend, Jessica Chin, works at Socrates Academy.

Becca nudges me. "What is he saying?"

"Something about the campus tour."

"That's all?" Becca turns away to pick up her backpack. "We really should go if we don't want to be late for school."

"In a minute," I say, still watching Leo's mouth.

"...thought it over...going to live..." Leo catches me staring at him and turns away—but not before I "hear" his shocking words.

Reeling, I grab on to the edge of a desk so I don't fall over.

"What is it?" Becca drops her backpack to grab my arm.

I gasp. "Leo's moving in with his father!"

- Chapter 10 -

Is Anyone There?

Leo clicks off his phone and walks over to us like everything is fine.

Words lump in my throat. I stare at him in shock.

But Becca plants her hands on her hips and gets in his face. "Seriously? You're just going to move away like your friends don't even matter? What's wrong with you?"

"How did you...?" Leo turns to look at me, accusingly. "Lipreading?"

I nod. "You were acting suspicious."

"It's unethical to use spy tactics on a club mate."

"It's not so great whispering when we're in the room with you either," I say, anger rising. "I make a motion that we take a club vote on whether you can leave. I vote no."

"I second the motion, and vote no," Becca says.

"Majority rules," I say with a lip-smack of satisfaction.

"You—you can't do that," Leo sputters. "This is my life."

"We're in a club, so this isn't all about you." Becca points her sparkly blue polished fingernail at Leo.

"Where I attend school isn't up for a vote."

I narrow my gaze at Leo. "Are you enrolling in that lah-de-dah fancy academy?"

"I have no plans to do that." Leo tucks his phone in his pocket.

"But you're thinking about it," I accuse. "You're going to tour the campus."

He nods. "Professor Chin wants to show us around. I've read the brochure, and they offer advanced programs for gifted students."

"That's perfect for you." I sigh, my heart breaking a little.

"Not perfect." He frowns. "But it would be beneficial to my education."

Becca scowls. "So you're moving away?"

"Nothing is decided. My mother doesn't want me to go, although she'll let me decide. My father says that Socrates Academy is the ideal place for a student with my abilities."

"And what do *you* want to do?" I hold my breath.

Leo, who is usually so sure of everything, shrugs. "I don't know. I don't want to leave, but I could learn so much at an advanced school."

"Well I think it sucks." Becca purses her peach-frosted lips. "The CCSC needs you."

"Frankie can take my place," he suggests.

I shake my head. "He's too busy with drama club. Besides he's not..." *You,* I think.

"There's no point in discussing this until I consider the pros and cons of switching schools." Leo sits in front of his computer, so his back is to us. "I've told my father I'll give him my decision after I tour the campus on Friday. According to my calculations, there's a 37 percent chance I won't even like Socrates Academy."

I don't have to be a genius to know those aren't great odds. And why wouldn't he want to go to a school with other smart kids like him? He'll probably become best friends with the clever professor's daughter and forget all about us.

I'm still stressing over Leo when I slip into homeroom a while later.

It's a very long short day at school for me. I can't concentrate on what my teachers are saying. I keep thinking about Leo. He just can't move away! He's my friend...maybe more than a friend. He invited me to a dance and to a robotics competition. We've had so much fun together solving mysteries and helping animals.

Is all that going to end?

There's no lunch break, so I only see Becca a few times passing in the halls, and I don't see Leo at all. When the final bell rings, I hurry out to the bike rack. Normally, I'd wait for my club mates, and we'd go to the Skunk Shack or ride around looking for lost pets. But not today.

Sometimes I think the weather knows my moods, because on my ride home the wind whips into a fury. My hair flies in my face, and I push it away. My thoughts chant Leo's name over and over. I pedal faster, trying to outrace my worries.

I can't imagine the Curious Cat Spy Club without Leo. It was his idea to start a club to help animals. He was the first one of us to keep one of the three kittens we rescued. Even if we promote our associate member, Frankie, to full member, the club won't be the same without Leo. He's a one-of-a-kind friend…and I'll miss him.

I slow when I near Lyric's house and peer down her private road. But I can't see even the roof of her house through the tangle of trees. Sighing, I continue pedaling, turning on my road and bump-bumping across the bridge to my house.

When I step inside, I inhale a faint odor of paint. I listen for sounds of life but only hear my own footsteps and the whooshing wind rattling windows. I don't expect anyone else to be home this early on a weekday. Chef Dad is cooking up a storm at Bragg Castle and Animal Control Officer Mom is out on calls. Since only the middle school has a short day, my siblings are still in school. It's weird being home alone.

But I'll have company soon.

My sneakers pound on the stairs as I hurry. I dump my backpack on my bed then check the food and water bowls for my pets. Honey rubs against my legs, purring, while Trixie hops around in her cage, wanting out to play. But she'll have to wait. I double-check her latch, adding a twist of wire so there's no way she can escape. No way is Hoppity Houdini getting out until I'm ready to show her to Lyric.

"You remember Lyric, don't you?" I poke my finger through the cage, and she nuzzles it. "She thinks you can lead us to a treasure. If you do, I'll give you extra veggie treats."

Soft fur brushes against my legs, and I smile down at my kitty. "You can go treasure hunting too," I tell Honey as I scoop her up in my arms. "Lyric's kind of unusual, but I like her. I'm hoping we can be real friends—not secret friends."

I set off to meet Lyric a few minutes later. Sunshine warms my face, but the wind is blustery. Loose hairs blow in my mouth, and I spit them out as I cut through the overgrown garden.

Glancing over at the large oak at the edge of my yard, all I see are tangled berry bushes. It's surprising how well the trail to the river is hidden. But it's easy to spot once I crawl around the large tree. The gaping hole is dark and empty.

"Lyric!" I call. But my voice is lost in the thorny branches.

I check my watch. Two minutes after one. Where is she?

I wait by the pump house, where I have a good view and the overhanging roof protects me from the wind. Leaning against a wall, I sit.

Minutes tick by. Five. Ten. Twenty.

Chilly wind howls around me, and I huddle closer to the wall. When a half hour has passed, I wonder if Lyric forgot our meeting. Or maybe she's sick. Why didn't I ask for her phone number?

By two o'clock, it's obvious she's not coming.

I ball my fists and grit my teeth. I gave up hanging out with my club mates for someone who can't even bother to show up. And she had the nerve to ask *me* to keep her a secret? Well, I'm done waiting.

The wind has grown fierce. I can barely walk across my yard without stumbling. I wrench open the front door, and it slams shut behind me. My footsteps on the stairs echo in my empty house. I usually love being alone but now it just seems lonely. Upstairs in my room, I flop on my bed and stare up at the stained ceiling.

Today really sucks. First I find out Leo might move away, and now I'm stood up by someone I hoped would become a friend.

Honey jumps up. I wrap my arm around her, drawing her to my chest. She purrs and curls up to sleep. Across the room in her hutch, Trixie is sleeping too. I yawn and pound my pillow so it tucks snugly under my neck. And like my animals, I drift to sleep...

I jerk awake so abruptly, my pillow tumbles onto the floor. Honey yowls, her fur bristling on end. For a moment, I'm confused about what woke me. And then I hear a faint tinkling like distant wind chimes.

Death bells? Like in Philomena's ghost story? Does that mean someone is going to die?

I shake away these crazy thoughts from my head. I must be still dreaming. But when I pinch myself, it hurts for real.

Where is the sound coming from? I dig my fingers into my covers, listening, trying to pinpoint the location of the bells. But it's gone.

My cat leaps from the bed and scampers over to the door. She flicks her tail back and forth, then jumps through the pet door.

"Honey, where—"

Bang! The sound echoes from downstairs.

Someone's in my house! It's too early for Mom, Dad, my sisters, or my brother to be home, although I guess it's possible. Still, I look around for a weapon to protect myself. The best I can find is a small broom used for sweeping around the rabbit hutch. It's not much longer than my arm, but holding it makes me feel safer.

Trying not to panic, I cross over to my window. I look down into the front yard for Mom's animal control truck, Dad's SUV, or my brother's second-hand Toyota. Our gravel driveway is empty. And my bike is the only one propped up by the porch.

Shivers slither up my spine.

I tiptoe over to the door and peek into the hallway. I don't see anyone. But at the top of the stairs, my cat sits like a guard dog, her bristling tail swishing furiously.

Holding my broom in one arm and my cat in the other, I start down the stairs. One step, two, three...

Bang! Thud!

The sound came from the living room right below me!

What should I do?

I can't get out of the house without going through the front or back doors—and both are downstairs. I can't call for help because I don't have a cell phone, and to get to the only phone—a landline in the kitchen—I'd have to cross through the living room.

Crash!

I jump at the sound of glass shattering.

Someone is definitely in my house!

I have to get out of here!

Since I can't go downstairs, I go up. Tucking the broom under my arm, I hold Honey so tightly she squirms, and I race down the hall to the spiral staircase to the third floor. My sneakers bang on the metal circular steps, even though I'm trying to move silently. When I reach the turret bedroom, I shut the door firmly. I twist the lock and check it to make sure it's secure.

Crossing over to the bay windows, I set Honey down on the window seat. Still gripping the broom, I press my face to the glass. My gaze sweeps from the empty driveway to the overgrown garden and the yard that ends at the wild blackberry cliff. I stare longingly at the large pine tree, wishing I could escape through the hidden trail and run for help.

Instead, I'm trapped like Rapunzel in a tower... well, turret.

Honey's purring is soothing, and I bury my face in her fur.

What should I do? I agonize. Will the intruder come upstairs looking for me? Or did he or she already leave? How long will I have to stay hidden?

Minutes stretch into eternities...

Finally, I can't take not knowing any longer. I cross over to my door. I release the lock and open it a crack. I don't see or hear anything. Honey squirms, wanting down. She's curious, like I am. But we have to be cautious.

I creep down the stairs. When I reach the second floor landing, I peer over the rail into the living room. Empty. Did the intruder leave?

I take a few steps down but pull back with a sharp cry when something white flutters like a ghost. But when I look closer, I sink with relief. Only a curtain, I realize with a shaky laugh. The narrow window in the back of the living room is wide open.

And another mystery is solved when I look below the window and see shattered remains of a glass vase and broken flowers scattered on the floor.

I blow out a breath, feeling silly. No intruder. It was just my imagination. Dad once teased that I could take a dripping faucet and turn it into a flood, and I guess he's right. There never was an intruder, only the wind banging an open window and knocking over a vase.

Honey runs back upstairs, probably going to nap after all the excitement. I'd like to join her, but there's work to do. I step around the broken glass to shut the window. I sweep up the broken glass onto a magazine then dump the mess in the garbage.

I go into the kitchen to use the phone. We really need to get an extension upstairs, I think. Or even better, maybe this will finally convince my parents to get me my own cell phone. Should I call to tell them about the open window? My sisters or brother probably forgot to close it. But I still have an uneasy feeling.

I really need to talk to my club mates. I hate breaking my promise to Lyric, but a real friend doesn't ask you to lie for them. Leo and Becca are my real friends, and they deserve the truth.

A huge weight lifts from me as I reach for the phone.

But who should I call? Leo? Becca? I'm trying to decide when I hear a thud.

I whirl around and...

No one is there.

A glance past the hallway shows sunlight streaming through the living room windows, all of them shut firmly. The room is silent.

Yet I hear a soft shuffling of footsteps.
I turn back toward the hallway—and scream!
A monstrous shadow flashes across the wall.

- Chapter 11 -
Intruder

I blink, and it's gone.

Did I really see a half-human shadow with whiskers and long ears? But there's nothing in the hall now. Am I imagining things?

I hear quick footsteps from the back of the house and a door slams shut.

Fear jolts through me.

Not my imagination!

If the sound is real, the shadow must be real, too. Yet it didn't look solid and seemed to float across the wall. Could it have been a ghost?

I want to be fearless like the heroines in the stories I read and dash off in brave pursuit, but my legs won't move. I don't know what is scarier—a ghost or an intruder?

Taking a deep breath, I try to think logically like Leo. He wouldn't panic; he'd analyze the facts until he came up with a realistic explanation. If ghosts and monsters don't exist (which I hope is true), that means someone was in my house.

Trembling, I rush into the kitchen and grab the phone.

Who should I call? If I describe the monstrous intruder to 911, they might think I'm pranking them. If I call my parents, they'll rush home to protect me—then never let me stay home alone again.

So I call Leo, because he lives closer than Becca… and well…I want to hear his voice.

"Polanski residence, Leo speaking," he answers, sounding so normal, for Leo anyway, that I immediately feel better.

"Someone was just in my house!" I blurt out.

He gasps. "Are you all right, Kelsey? Did you call 911?"

"No, I called you." I peer uneasily around the kitchen. "Because…well…it might have been a ghost."

"Highly unlikely. What exactly did you see?"

"A huge beastly shape floating down the hall."

"Could it have been a shadow?" he says. "A shadow occurs when a light source is blocked by an opaque object."

"There were footsteps and other strange sounds." I glance nervously through the elegant curved archway that opens from the kitchen into the hall. "But I'm the only one here."

"Why are you alone? You told us you were meeting with someone after school," he says, accusingly.

"I'll tell you about that later," I say with an uneasy glance around the room. "Freaky things are happening. I fell asleep in my room and suddenly woke to the sound of bells—like the death bells in Philomena's ghost story."

"Are you sure you weren't dreaming?"

"I know when I'm awake," I snap. "Philomena said my house was haunted, and I'm starting to believe her."

"*Au contraire*," Leo insists. "Even if I consider the theory that ghosts exist, an incorporeal body wouldn't have the substance to make footstep sounds."

"Incorpor—what?" I shake the phone to make sure I'm hearing right.

"It means to have no material body or form," Leo spouts off like a dictionary. "All evidence points to a human intruder who came in through the window and left through the back door."

I squeeze my fingers around the phone. "What if he's still here?"

"Unlikely. Your scream probably scared him as much as he scared you. He's long gone by now," Leo assures me. "Still, you need to call Sheriff Fischer. And lock all the doors until I get there."

"You're coming over?" My heart jumps in a good way. Leo sounds worried, like he really cares about me. Of course, we're friends, and friends do care about each other.

Hanging up the phone, I glance nervously around the kitchen.

Leo said to lock the doors, so I go to the front door and twist the lock shut. Honey pads loyally behind me as I go to the back door, her fur no longer bristling. Once the doors are secure, I return to the kitchen to call the sheriff. Since he's Mom's boss, his number is listed on a printed sheet of important numbers fixed to the refrigerator with a magnet.

Sheriff Fischer must have zoomed through streets with his sirens blasting, because I am not exaggerating when I say he arrives in less than five minutes. His truck tires skid on our driveway, and I run outside to meet him.

"I told you to wait inside," he barks. He looks tough and rough with broad shoulders, deep lines on his middle-aged face, and a no-nonsense expression. His voice softens as he asks, "Are you all right, Kelsey?"

"Yeah, just freaked out." I bite my lip. "I heard scary sounds and saw something strange."

"Strange?" His hat tips forward as he leans toward me. "What exactly?"

"A dark shape in the hall." I pause, not wanting to sound crazy by calling it part animal and part human. "Then I heard footsteps and the back door closing."

"Probably a homeless person seeking shelter from the wind, who assumed the house was still empty. I'll look around." He bends to look into my face. "Have you called your parents?"

"Do I have to?" I cringe. "I don't want to upset them."

He arches a dark brow. "So you called me instead?"

"Actually, I called Leo first," I admit with a wry smile. "He told me to call you."

"Smart boy, that Leo. He has a good head on his shoulders," he says fondly. "You did the right thing by calling me. But you still need to call your parents." He sweeps his gaze around the yard and house as if he's seeing every direction at once. "While you do that, I'll check around the house."

Drats. I really don't want to tell Mom and Dad. But there's no room for no when Sheriff Fischer gives an order. So I go back into the kitchen and pick up the phone.

When Dad finishes shouting at me for not calling him first (I called Mom and she's on her way home), I join the sheriff in the back of the house. He shines a flashlight on the doorknob.

"Are you going to dust for fingerprints?" I ask, thinking of the fingerprinting tools in my spy pack upstairs.

He grins. "How about you let me ask the questions? Tell me exactly happened from the beginning."

"I got out of school early and—" I hesitate, not wanting to mention Lyric. "I was tired, so I went upstairs to rest in my room—well, not *my* room, just the one I share with my sisters until my bedroom is fixed up."

He scribbles in a notebook. "You were alone?" he asks.

"Yeah...except for my bunny and cat." I gesture to Honey who sits quietly by my feet. "I was sleepy, so I took a nap. But strange sounds woke me up..." I launch into the timeline of events. I don't mention Lyric, though, since there's no reason to get her in trouble.

"So let me get this straight." The sheriff looks up from his notebook, studying me like I'm the topic for a pop quiz. "You woke up because you heard noises?"

"Like tinkling bells, but we don't have wind chimes." I shudder. "There was a thud too, and shattering glass. I ran downstairs and found the window open and a broken vase."

"It's windy today, so the wind probably knocked over the vase," he suggests.

"Yeah, that's what I thought—until I was in the kitchen. I heard footsteps and a door slam."

"Where were the sounds coming from?"

"The hallway, between the kitchen and the living room," I point down the hall. "I also saw a dark shape rush by."

"A man or woman?"

"Um...I'm not sure. Leo thinks I probably saw a shadow of the intruder."

Sheriff Fischer nods, scribbling in his notebook. His neutral expression gives nothing away. If I told him I might have seen a ghost, would he believe me?

When he tucks his notebook in a back pocket and reaches out to pat my hand, his expression softens. "There's nothing to worry about, Kelsey. If someone was here, they're gone now. But I'll search inside the house as a precaution. Stay in the kitchen and wait."

I wait for about ten minutes, until I hear a whirring sound from outside.

Leo is here!

Setting my glass on the counter, I race to the door. I'm so glad to see Leo that I could hug him. But my face reddens at this thought and I shift backward.

"I saw the sheriff's truck."

"His truck is faster than your gyro-board. He already searched outside, and he's upstairs now making sure no one is here. I was ordered to wait in the kitchen, so come with me."

As Leo follows me through the hall, he pauses when we reach the living room and points. "Which window was open?"

"The one in the back, facing the garden...well, the weeded patch that will be a garden when Mom has time to work on it," I add. "The vase that broke was full of wild flowers Mom picked."

"And where did you see the shadow?"

"It was more than a shadow," I snap, annoyed that he won't even consider the possibility of a ghost. "After Caroline heard death bells and saw a ghost, she drowned."

"You wouldn't be foolish enough to wander outside and jump into a swift river," he says matter-of-factly. "Besides, there's no easy access to the river from your house."

There's the hidden berry-covered path, I think, but I don't tell him because his know-it-all attitude rubs me like petting a cat's fur the wrong direction.

Leo drums his fingers on the table and clears his throat. "I have some good news," he says.

"What?" I lean forward in my chair.

"Dad and Professor Chin have volunteered to help at the dog wash."

"Great," I say, although I'm not feeling great about seeing the people who want Leo to move away. "Is the professor's daughter coming too?"

"Brilliant suggestion!" Leo snaps his fingers. "I hadn't thought to ask Riley, but I will now. Thanks for the idea, Kelsey."

I want to smack myself in the head. Why couldn't I keep my big mouth shut?

Before I can comment, I hear tires on the cracked pavement outside.

The door bursts open. Mom rushes in first, wearing her animal control uniform, with Dad right behind her. He's wearing a chef's apron that reads *One Day I'm Going to Make Onions Cry.* They surround me with hugs and questions. Once I convince them I wasn't attacked or hurt in any way, I explain what happened. I downplay the danger so they don't overreact and forbid me to ever be alone again.

Mom strangles me in a hug. "I'm so glad you're safe."

"I'm fine," I assure them. "It might have just been the wind."

"Possibly," the sheriff says as he enters the room. He tucks the notebook he was jotting on into a pocket. "The wind could have broken the vase. I checked the window, and it doesn't show any sign of forced entry."

"Kenya is terrible about shutting doors. She probably left the window open." Mom seems more businesslike than momlike as she talks to the sheriff because he is her boss. "Did you inspect the doors and search outside for footprints?"

His cap slips down to his bushy dark brows as he nods. "All checked out, Katherine. No evidence of an intruder."

"What about the inside of the house?" Mom persists. "Did you look upstairs?"

"I checked every room." Sheriff Fischer nods. "Nothing suspicious. The only living thing I saw was that orange cat sleeping on a bed."

"And a bunny," I add.

The sheriff gives me a funny look. "What bunny?"

"She's in a cage in my bedroom."

He shakes his head. "I looked in that cage, but it was empty."

- Chapter 12 -
Bunny-Napped

How could Trixie escape a locked cage?

The latch even has a twist of wire around the bars for extra security. Trixie couldn't have gotten out of the cage on her own. Someone—or *something*—took her.

But why would anyone steal a bunny?

My parents and the sheriff fire questions at me about Trixie, but it's hard to talk when I'm trying not to cry. Shine a hot lamp on me and call me guilty, because I blame myself. I think back to the last time I saw Trixie, after I heard glass shatter. I'd scooped up Honey to protect her, but it never occurred to me that Trixie needed protection too.

Instead of taking her to safety, I left her alone. And now she's gone.

The sheriff apologizes because he has to go on another call and can't stay to search for the bunny. "But take the rest of the afternoon off, Katherine," he kindly tells Mom. "A bunny clever enough to escape a locked cage will come back when she's hungry. Let me know when you find her," he adds, optimistically.

As the sheriff drives out of our yard, Becca whirls in on her bike, her pink-black ponytail whipping in the gusty wind. She's changed out of the leopard-print dress she wore to school and into the jeans and worn T-shirt she wears when working in animal pens and stalls.

"Leo texted, so I came ASAP." She hops off her bike and gives me a hug. "I'm sorry I didn't get here sooner, but the bear cub cut his foot and I helped Mom bandage it. Leo said there was an intruder. Are you okay?"

"I'm okay, but Trixie isn't." I gulp back tears. I explain what happened as Leo and I lead her upstairs to my room.

"Evidence A." Leo points to the empty cage. "The bunny is gone, yet the cage is latched shut."

"And the wire is still there too," I add, feeling sick inside. "Trixie may be tricky, but even if she opened the cage, she couldn't lock it after she escaped."

"Puzzling." Leo rubs his chin. "A lop-eared bunny is an odd target for a thief."

Becca frowns. "Who would take her?"

I can think of only one person. Lyric's clue jumps into my head: *Follow the bunny.* But why would Lyric steal Trixie when I invited her to my house? We could have followed the clue together.

My heart aches as I confess. "I think I know who has Trixie."

"Who?" Leo asks, surprised.

I hesitate. "The girl I saw by the river."

"The one with a magic wand?" Becca teases.

"Not a wand—a fishing pole that's retractable. Her name is Lyric, and she's my neighbor." I gesture in the direction of her home. "I talked to her yesterday, and she told me how she used to hang out with the old woman who lived here. The woman made up games for Lyric with clues leading to a prize. But the woman died suddenly, and Lyric never got a chance to finish her last game."

Becca puts her hands on her hips. "And you're just telling us this *now*?"

"You didn't believe me when I first told you about Lyric," I remind her. "Besides, she made me promise not to tell. She was going to come over today to search—only she never showed up. She went back on her word, so I'm not keeping her a secret anymore. I'm glad I can finally tell you."

Leo folds his arms. "Honest individuals do not request anonymity."

Becca nods. "Whatever he said, I agree. She doesn't sound like a good friend."

"She seemed nice. But she wasn't supposed to be at my house—that's why she didn't want me to tell anyone we'd met. She was afraid of getting in trouble again." I quickly explain about Lyric's run-in with Sheriff Fischer.

"Sheriff Fischer isn't her enemy," Becca scoffs. "He was nice to take her home. I'll bet she was lying to trick you into inviting her into your house."

"She showed me the clue, and it was cursive like an adult would write. Besides, why would she lie?"

"Isn't it obvious?" Becca snaps her fingers. "So she can search your house for *real* treasure."

I shake my head. "Lyric doesn't believe the rumors of treasure."

Leo leans into the conversation. "Your house has been vacant for over two years. Why wait to search for her prize until now?"

"She couldn't follow the bunny when Trixie was living at our realtor's house." I stare gloomily at the empty cage. "I actually hope Trixie is with Lyric—at least that means she's safe. I keep imagining her lost outside, hurt and hungry and scared."

"We'll find her," Becca assures, patting my hand.

"I hope so." I sniff. "She's so sweet and really smart. I never would have found the old key if she hadn't led me to the hidden panel."

Leo tilts his head thoughtfully. "Could the key be Lyric's prize?"

I shrug. "Not a very good one."

"That depends on what it opens." Leo's blue eyes gleam excitedly. "Perhaps it's the key to real treasure."

I fold my arms skeptically. "If there *is* a treasure."

"I'm going to find out," he says with a determined expression.

Before I can ask what he's planning, the bedroom door bursts open.

It's my parents.

"The bunny really is gone." Dad stares into the empty cage, his face wrinkled with worry lines. "Kelsey, how could this happen?"

"I don't know," I say, not wanting to blame Lyric without proof. "The metal bars are too close together for Trixie to slip through. And the cage door is firmly latched and locked."

"This is a disaster!" Dad runs his fingers through his dark hair. "We have to find her."

I stare at Dad in surprise. "I didn't think you liked Trixie."

"My feelings have nothing to do with this situation. I signed a legal paper promising to care for the bunny as long as she lived. I will protect that floppy-eared nuisance if it kills me—and it might." Gripping the bars of the cage, he groans. "How could a tiny animal create such a big problem?"

"We'll find her." Mom lays a calming hand on Dad's shoulder. "Unless whoever broke into our house took her—which seems highly unlikely—she's around here somewhere. Let's organize a search."

Becca, Leo, and I start with the second floor. I grab my spy pack from its hidden spot in the closet and put on my flash cap and plastic gloves.

"My phone is my flashlight," Becca says, tapping

the screen. She aims the bright light underneath my sister Kenya's bed.

Dropping to the floor, I shine my flash cap under the bed. Cobwebs, a candy bar wrapper, and three socks that don't match.

I hear an odd humming, and look over to the far side of the room where Leo holds a small square device to the wall.

"What are you doing, Leo?" I call out. "You're supposed to be looking for Trixie."

"I'm employing my more advanced search skills with my radar indicator," he says.

"Leaving us to do the dirty work," I complain.

"You and Becca are doing an excellent job."

Becca peers over his shoulder. "That contraption can see through walls?"

"Absolutely. It can identify solid objects behind a wall, such as a lost rabbit or a treasure."

"Like with super-vision?" I wipe off dust from my jeans then come up beside Leo for a closer look.

"Nothing supernatural—it's basic science. The indicator has multiple settings for an accurate reading." Leo holds out a device the size of a cell phone. The screen shows a blob of orange, a line of purple, and a black dot that flickers—until the screen goes blank.

"What happened?" I frown. "Is it broken?"

"No." Leo taps buttons. "The power source malfunctioned."

"If your supermachine won't work, we can use your help searching the low-tech way." Becca brushes cat hair off her jeans. "Get down on your knees and help us check under the bed."

"Never doubt the reliability of a machine," Leo assures us as the supervision device hums and flashes. He turns back to the wall, and Becca and I drop back down to the floor. We look in every box, under chairs and beds—but no bunny.

Downstairs, banging, voices, and footsteps echo through the house. My sisters and brother are home from school. Soon they're searching for Trixie, too.

But hours later, Trixie is still missing.

As dusk sets, Becca and Leo have to leave, but they promise to come back tomorrow to search again.

I'm surer than ever that Lyric took Trixie. Still, there's a chance Trixie is lost outside. So I tromp through high weeds and look in outbuildings. When I hear a rustling behind the shed, my heart jumps with hope.

"Here bunny, bunny," I call hopefully.

The weeds sway and I tiptoe over. Pulling back tall grass, I see a wiggle of brown ears and exclaim, "Trixie!"

A wild jackrabbit—four times the size of a mini-lop bunny—leaps away.

Sighing, I return to the house. My family is weary and discouraged too—especially Dad. He lives to cook, yet he's so upset, he orders out for pizza.

Before I go to bed that night, I fill a small dish with rabbit food.

I leave it outside on the front step.

Just in case.

First thing the next morning, I check the bunny cage, crossing my fingers Trixie's back in her straw nest. But the cage remains empty.

So I dress quickly and start outside to search for her—until Mom sees me.

I beg Mom to let me skip school so I can search for Trixie. She gives me a firm, "No way."

My mood sucks bitter lemons as I enter my homeroom class. I just want school to be over already so I can resume my search.

As I slump into my chair, Becca turns around furtively and slips me a note.

CCSC will find Trixie after school. <3

I reach across my desk to squeeze Becca's shoulder and whisper, "Thank you."

While I half listen to my teachers the rest of the morning, I puzzle over Trixie's disappearance. There are three logical explanations.

Trixie is hiding inside the house.

Trixie is lost outside the house.

Trixie was bunny-napped.

The only evidence that she's outside is the empty rabbit food dish I found this morning. Of course, the wild rabbit I saw might have eaten the food. And when I searched the house again, there was no evidence, like rabbit poo, to prove Trixie was here.

While other kids are doing assigned reading, I try to think of more places to search for Trixie. Maybe the attic? But unless bunnies can fly, there's no way Trixie could pull down the ceiling ladder. There's also the old bomb shelter, but my parents keep it locked and bolted closed. Not even Tricky Trixie could get through solid cement.

I'm pondering bunny hiding places as I walk into the cafeteria at lunch break. I hear raised voices and laughter, and notice a large crowd surrounding the Sparklers table.

What's going on?

I'm too short to see over heads, but small enough to squeeze through the crowd. When I get close enough, I spot Becca sitting between blue-haired Sophia and spiky-haired drama-girl Chloe. Tyla is the starring attraction, showing her admirers a glittering green puffball.

Not a puffball—but a tiny poodle.

A glittery green poodle.

"Isn't she the sweetest darling?" I hear a girl croon.

"Green fur is gorgeous!" someone else says.

"You're so talented, Tyla!" another girl gushes. "How did you do it?"

"I gave her my special Sparkler Beautification Treatment. It's food coloring so it doesn't hurt the animal and comes in multiple colors. If purple is your favorite color, you can have a purple dog. Come to the animal shelter fund-raiser on Saturday, and I'll beautify your dogs, too!" Tyla says in a loud voice like she's advertising on a shopping channel.

Tyla is so over-the-top annoying, I want to vomit. A dog should *not* be green or purple.

But the others love it. Tyla hands out flyers, inviting kids to bring their dogs for a beautification treatment on Saturday. Becca catches my gaze with a shrug as if to say, "It's all for a good cause."

The Tyla shopping channel would have lasted longer, but the lunch lady—actually a man with an eye patch and beard like a pirate—ordered Tyla to take her dog outside. I almost applaud when he announces that animals in a cafeteria are unsanitary and not allowed. You tell her, Mr. Lunch Lady!

Still, I sink into a bad mood, wondering if Lyric's bad luck is contagious. That's the only kind of luck I've had lately. Leo may move away, my bunny is missing, and our dog washing fund-raising booth will probably have zero customers because "beautification treatment" sounds more glamorous than soapy water.

When I go to the bike rack after school, Becca is waiting. Right away, she notices my rotten mood.

"Still worrying about Trixie?" she asks, unlocking her bike.

"Yeah." I sigh. "I keep hoping that when I get home, she'll be there. But I don't see how she could have gotten out of her cage on her own—unless someone took her."

"Probably Lyric. We should go over there right now and confront her," Becca says, hopping on her bike. "We'll demand she return the bunny and refuse to leave until she does."

"You're so fierce when it comes to protecting animals." I roll my bike out of the rack. "Like a superhero."

"Heroine," she corrects. "All I need is a Super Pet Protector cape."

I imagine her in an animal-print supersuit with cape and laugh for the first time today. Becca always knows how to cheer me up.

I hear a whirring sound, and Leo rolls up on his gyro-board.

"We're going to Lyric's house to rescue Trixie," I explain to him. "Let's get rolling!"

Instead of clicking the power button on his gyro-board, he shakes his head. "Not yet."

"Why not?" I wheel my bike around so I face him.

"There's somewhere else I'd like to go first. I made an important discovery."

I clutch my hands together hopefully. "About Trixie?"

"No, not about the bunny—about treasure. I researched Jacoby Whitney to determine whether the rumors of treasure are true. According to my calculations, there's a 78 percent chance the treasure is an urban myth. There's no record of any treasure. I was ready to quit."

Quit is not in my vocabulary. Besides, I heard the ghostly bells and saw the creepy dark shadow. If that part of Philomena's story is true, the treasure must be real too.

"But then I found a list of the girls who attended Caroline's birthday party," Leo continues, lowering his tone as a group of kids grab their bikes from the rack.

"Coolness!" Becca grins.

I balance my bike beside me. "But won't those girls be old women by now?"

"Yes, they're nonagenarians." He seems to notice our confusion. "That's the term for people in their nineties. I found out one of them lives near my house."

"What's her name?" Becca shifts her backpack on her shoulders.

"Marjorie Ann Stephens."

"Marjorie Ann was Caroline's best friend!" I bounce excitedly. "If anyone knows about the treasure, she will."

"That's why I want to interview her right away," Leo says as he powers up his gyro-board. "It's on the way to Lyric's house. And it will only take a few minutes to talk to her."

"Well...all right." I purse my lips. "But afterward, we rescue Trixie."

Becca and I hop on our bikes, and we roll away from school. When we stop at a crosswalk, I turn to Leo. "What's the address?"

"351 Blossom Street," he shouts to be heard over noisy kids crossing the street.

He zooms ahead, and I pedal quickly to catch up, taking the same route as if we were going to his house. I've gone down Blossom Street many times searching for lost pets. I know some of the people who live here, although mostly I know their pets. Punky, an orange cat, shared by the four Wyckoff kids; Duke, a Great Pyrenees, who looks intimidating but is super lovable; and Siamese cats sharing a home with several college students.

Up ahead is a familiar house I've visited many times. Golden stalks of flowers bloom up to the front porch where Sunflower Mary creaks back and forth in her rocking chair. I met her when the CCSC was following clues to solve a puzzling zorse mystery.

Leo abruptly stops in front of a yard of blooming sunflowers, and I almost fall off my bike. "This can't be the right house!"

"But it is." Leo nods, looking as shocked as I feel.

Sunflower Mary is Marjorie Ann!

- Chapter 13 -
Yarn-Ado

Sunflower Mary is a living monument in Sun Flower. She's a tiny wrinkled woman with sharp black eyes and gaudy necklaces jangling on her blouse. Everyone knows her, and she knows secrets about the people in town. Before she hurt her hip and had to use a cane, she'd walk around downtown giving away crocheted sunflower pins. Now she spends her days rocking on her front porch, crocheting golden flowers.

As we roll into her driveway, she calls out, "Help! Help!"

In a flash, Leo is off his gyro-board, and Becca and I drop our bikes on the grass. We rush to the porch through a path shaded by sunflowers.

"Thank goodness you're here!" Sunflower Mary sobs.

I come up beside her. "Are you hurt?"

Becca gently touches the old woman's arm. "Should we call a doctor?"

"I'm fine. But my yarn is a disaster." She gestures to a pile of tangled yarn. "The neighbor's cats got into my craft bag, and now a dozen balls of yarn are one hopeless blob."

"What a mess." Becca frowns as she surveys the twisted yarn. "It's like a tornado ripped through the yarn."

"A yarn-ado," I tease.

Leo blinks. "Huh? That's not a word."

"If the word fits, use it," Sunflower Mary says, then groans. "My yarn is ruined. And I promised to crochet a hundred flowers for the Sunny Garden Club by this weekend. What am I going to do?"

"We'll unravel it." I give my club mates a meaningful look. Aside from helping a friend, this is our chance to question her about Caroline Whitney.

I kneel down on the wood porch and start unraveling yellow yarn and rolling it into a neat ball. Becca and Leo do the same.

Sunflower Mary reaches into her craft bag and takes out purple yarn and a gold crochet hook. Her chair creaks as she rocks back and forth, crocheting a chain of yarn. This is my chance to ask her about Caroline Whitney. But my tongue feels thick in my mouth, like words are an obstacle course that I might trip over. I look over at Becca, who's a social expert, for help but she's busy untying knots.

Turning to Sunflower Mary, I blurt out, "I met someone who went to school with you."

"You did?" She stops rocking. "Not many of them are still around. Who?"

"Philomena Dansbury."

She stares at me blankly then slowly smiles. "Oh, you mean Silly Philly."

Becca frowns. "Why did you call her that?"

"I suppose the nickname sounds cruel now, but back then we all had nicknames. Philly was always day-dreaming and didn't talk much except to tell wild stories."

"What sort of stories?" I ask.

"Most of her stories were nonsense—aliens, invisible friends, fairies. But I do remember one..." She leans on her cane with a gaze that seems to travel back in time. "She came to school wearing a crown

154

of seashells. She told us she was really a mermaid, trapped in a human body by a magical spell."

"Like the movie *The Little Mermaid*," Becca says.

Sunflower Mary shakes her head. "Philly always had her nose in a book, so she probably got the idea from the original *The Little Mermaid*."

"Written by the Danish author Hans Christian Andersen in the 1800s," Leo adds.

"Yes," the old lady nods, looking impressed. "When Philly described the ocean as cornflower blue and crystal clear, I fell under the spell of her words. I wanted to believe in magic and mermaids. But everyone knew Philly made things up." Sunflower Mary taps her cane on the wooden porch. "Caro used to say that Philly lived in a fantasy world."

"Caro?" I perk with interest. "Do you mean Caroline Whitney?"

"How do you know about her?" She narrows her faded brows at me. "What did Silly...I mean, Philomena...tell you?"

"Not much. Just that she went to Caroline's birthday party." I pause winding my yarn to look at her curiously. "But if Caroline didn't like her, why invite her to the party?"

"All the girls in our class were invited because it would have been rude to exclude anyone. It was such a lovely party, and I had a wonderful time until..." Her words trail off like the dangling yarn.

"Philomena told me Caroline drowned," I say with a sad shake of my head.

"Caro was my best friend ever...and losing her was hard."

I can tell she's going to stop talking, so I blurt out, "Do you still have your toy bunny?"

Sunflower Mary rocks back with surprise, her crochet hook falling.

Leo swoops down for a swift catch and returns the hook.

"Thanks, young man," she says, but her gaze stays on me. "So Philly told you about the toy bunnies?"

"She showed me hers."

Sunflower Mary's gray brows rise. "She still has that old thing?"

"Yes. She keeps it in a glass case, next to a photo from Caroline's party. Her nephew is our realtor. We just moved into the old house that Caroline used to live in, and Philomena told us it was haunted."

"So that's why you've been asking all these questions." She idly turns the golden hook in her hand, her lips pursed so I can't tell if she's amused or angry. "I've seen Philly and her nephew around town, but I don't know them well. It's easier not to bring up sad memories, so I rarely talk of Caro. But since you rescued my yarn, I'll show you something I haven't shown anyone in over sixty years."

"The toy bunny?" Becca asks hopefully.

"No. That cheap copy of the original fell apart decades ago, so I threw it away." She cracks a wry smile. "But I have a photograph of Caroline and me. Would you like to see it?"

Becca, Leo, and I nod eagerly.

Sunflower Mary reaches for her cane, but the sudden movement makes her groan. "My hip is acting up again."

Leo hops up. "I'll get the photo for you. Where is it?"

"That's kind of you, young man. I can't move as easily as I used to." She rubs her hip. "The photograph is on the mantle above the fireplace in the living room."

Leo hurries into the house. Minutes pass with each creak of the rocking chair, and I grow impatient. The ball of yarn in my hands is now the size of an apple. Becca's is even larger. I glance at my watch and frown. What is keeping Leo?

The door bursts open. Leo holds a framed photograph that looks heavy and very old. As he hands it to Philomena, he sneaks a meaningful glance at me and Becca. His blue eyes sparkle excitedly like there's something he wants to tell us. But he only mouths, "Later."

What could he have discovered? I'm dying to ask him.

"Come look," the old woman says. "Caroline was as lovely as she was sweet."

Becca and I set aside our yarn balls and gather around for a close look at the photo. It's black and white and shows two girls with their arms around each other. They're about ten years old and wearing what must be school uniforms: dark jackets, white shirts with dark ties, and long pleated skirts. Although they're younger than they were in the photo Philomena showed me, I recognize them: Marjorie Ann has a plain face with a sharp nose and a long dark braid, while Caroline is petite with light curly hair pulled away from her heart-shaped face. They're grinning like someone just told a hilarious joke.

"Love the ties and jackets," Becca says. "Vintage clothes are very chic."

"And *very* uncomfortable," Sunflower Mary says with a grimace. "Clothes back then were stiff and had to be ironed almost every day. Girls weren't allowed to wear pants to school. But after school, Caro and I would switch into our dungarees—like your jeans—and pick berries or climb trees. We had so much fun together." She smiles sadly. "Times may change, but friendships are always important. I'm sure you three have fun together."

"We do." I pause, deciding to be honest. "Lately we've been searching for treasure. We heard that Caroline's father hid something valuable in my family's house. What do you know about it?"

"Not much. But I know plenty about Mr. Whitney— most of it bad." Her dark eyes flash angrily. "You do *not* want to hear my opinion of him."

"Actually, we do," Becca admits with a wicked grin.

"Especially if it helps us find the treasure," I add. "If there is one."

"Oh, there is," she says, which surprises me. "That despicable man valued money and possessions more than his own family. He was selfish, greedy, and cruel—especially to Caro."

Becca gasps, and Leo's mouth falls open. I realize my mouth is hanging open too and quickly shut it.

"In public he pretended to be a loving father, but Caroline was terrified of him." Sunflower Mary shudders. "When his wife left him, he got revenge by bribing a judge for custody of Caro. He gave Caro everything money could buy, but Caro only wanted her mother. Her father refused to even let them visit. He had a vile temper and took it out on Caro. If she didn't behave perfectly, he'd lock her in her room or threaten to hurt Trixie."

Becca's eyes widen. "Would he have really hurt the bunny?"

"Absolutely. He was heartless. But he paid for it later in life." She ties a crocheted chain into a small circle. "After he lost Caro, he traveled around the world selling fine glassware. I've seen his cabinets filled with lovely china and crystal. But he died bankrupt, and the cabinets were empty. Rumors about a hidden treasure spread. But no one knows what really happened." The old woman smiles slyly as she crochets another purple chain. "For decades treasure-seekers have searched the house but found nothing. I'm not surprised they all failed," she adds with a chuckle. "A greedy man tunnels his possessions away."

"Do you know where?" I ask in excitement.

"If I did, I'd be living in a mansion and wearing diamonds instead of costume jewelry." She jangles the bright beads around her neck. "I'm content with my cozy house and would rather make gifts for others than be rich." She holds out three purple yarn bracelets. "These friendship bracelets are for each of you."

"So that's what you were crocheting." I slip the bracelet over my wrist. "The yarn is so soft."

"And it has specks of glitter." Becca grins.

Leo looks down uncertainly at the bracelet. "Thank you," he says politely.

"You're welcome. When I first saw you three together, I knew you had a special friendship— much like I did with Caro," she says. "Friendship has a value that's priceless."

I smile at my friends. And the purple bracelet sparkles even though there's only a hint of sunlight through the darkening clouds.

We wave good-bye to Sunflower Mary and roll off down the street. As soon as we turn a corner and can no longer see sunflowers, Leo shouts "stop!" and powers off his gyro-board. Becca and I brake abruptly.

"I made an important discovery!" he exclaims

"Something you saw in the house?" I say, remembering his excited behavior after he returned with the photograph.

He nods. "After I picked up the photo from the mantle, my hands were dusty. So I went down a hall and opened the door I thought went to a bathroom, only it was a bedroom. And on the bed, I saw something shocking."

"What?" Becca and I both gasp.

And I hold my breath, waiting for Leo's answer.

Chapter 14

Dragon Flying

"A bunny," Leo announces.

"No way!" I almost fall off my bike. "Sunflower Mary has no reason to steal Trixie, and she can barely move without her cane!"

"Not *that* bunny." Leo gives us a pained look. "The bunny I saw wasn't alive; it was stuffed."

"The toy from Caroline's party?" Becca guesses.

"I can't be positive, but it matches Kelsey's description."

I scrunch my brow. "She told us she didn't have it anymore, that it fell apart and she threw it away."

"She lied," Leo says in an accusing tone.

"I don't believe it." I shake my head. "It must be a different bunny."

"Look for yourself." Leo holds out his cell phone. "Evidence A: picture proof."

I balance my bike with one hand and study the photo. There's no mistaking the brown and white floppy-eared toy. It's identical to the one I saw in Philomena's house—except it's in better shape. The faux fur shines, the necklace is a deep ruby red, and the bunny's black button eyes shimmer as if alive.

"For a toy she said was in such bad shape, the bunny looks new," Becca says. "She took really good care of it."

"If she didn't want us to see it, she could have just said so." I sigh. "Why lie about a dumb bunny?"

Leo shrugs. "Most human behavior baffles me."

I frown down at the purple bracelet on my wrist. "I thought she was my friend."

"She is your friend." Becca pats my shoulder. "Maybe talking about the bunny makes her sad because it reminds her of Caroline."

"She didn't have any problem showing us the photo and answering our questions about Caroline's father," I point out.

"Her information was interesting—especially when she said the treasure was real," Leo says.

"According to my calculations, there's a 73 percent possibility the treasure is hidden in the house."

"Or *under* the house!" A wild idea shapes into a real possibility. "Sunflower Mary must know more than she told us. She was Caroline's best friend, so she probably knows all the hiding places around my house. I thought it was odd when she said 'A greedy man tunnels his possessions away.' But what if it was a clue to the treasure?"

"A tunnel?" Becca's dark eyes go round.

Leo taps his chin thoughtfully. "The entrance must be hidden very well to go undiscovered for over eighty years. The odds of finding it are minimal."

"The CCSC has beaten the odds before and we can do it again," I say. A chilly wind tosses my hair, and the darkening sky hints at rain. "But I can't stop worrying about Trixie. I don't want to think Lyric is a thief, but I'm hoping we find her at Lyric's house."

"Let's stop at my house first since it's on the way so I can take a drone for surveillance." Leo rolls ahead of us on his gyro-board.

"Good idea," I say. "A drone can see into places that we can't."

"Yeah, like windows and fenced yards," Becca agrees as she hops on her bike. "If Trixie is there, we'll find her."

"She has to be." I cling to this hope. No one else has a reason to take Trixie. At least no one living, I think with a shudder as I remember the monstrous shape on the wall. I don't want to believe my house is haunted. But something huge and scary made that shadow.

And I wonder, can a ghost steal a bunny?

Leo zooms ahead and turns a corner. Becca and I catch up with him at his house and wait in the driveway. A minute later he returns, holding his drone case.

It doesn't take long before we turn onto River Road. We almost miss Lyric's driveway because it's cocooned deep in the woods and hidden by towering trees. We hide our bikes behind a huge bush and continue on foot.

When we're close enough to see the peaked roof, we duck behind a bush with red flowers. The only sounds are birds chirping and the wind whistling through the trees. I inhale the smell of freshly mowed grass as my gaze sweeps from the house to the detached garage. The driveway is empty and all the windows are darkened, like the house is sleeping.

"The absence of vehicles suggests that the dwelling is vacant," Leo says.

Becca nods. "I don't think anyone is home."

"Their motor home is gone." Realization dawns on me. "So that's why Lyric didn't show up! Her family went somewhere, probably because their band is performing out of town. If she left suddenly, that explains why she didn't meet with me."

"Band?" Becca pushes her dark bangs from her face.

"The whole family performs all over the country," I say, then quickly explain about Peanut Butter and Jamboree.

"Seriously?" Becca giggles. "Who names their band after food?"

"It's more common than you may think," Leo pipes up in his know-it-all tone. "The Black Eyed Peas, Smashing Pumpkins, Cake, Bread, Meat Loaf, Red Hot Chili—"

"Enough!" I raise my hand like a stop sign.

"—Peppers," Leo finishes with a grin.

Rolling my eyes, I turn back to Becca. "Anyway, it's a country music band, and the whole family is involved. Lyric says she can't sing very well, so she plays a tambourine. At least now I know why she didn't show up yesterday. But I wish she had told me."

"She probably didn't have time," Becca says.

"She must have left while I was in school yesterday. She doesn't know my house phone number, and it's not like I have a cell number to give her. But this means Lyric didn't take Trixie," I say, feeling lighter without the weight of suspicions. "I'm glad she isn't a thief."

Leo purses his lips skeptically. "Don't be so quick to cross her off the suspect list."

"Why not?"

"Your trip theory is logical, but her behavior is still suspicious. She's the only one with a motive to steal your bunny."

"It's not her fault if she had to leave on tour with her family."

"If that's what really happened. I need proof." Leo takes his phone from his pocket and taps the screen.

"What are you looking up?" Becca peers over Leo's shoulder.

"The music group Peanut Butter and—here it

is!" he exclaims. "Their website lists their events... April, May. No events scheduled this week."

"Of course not. Lyric didn't know she was going anywhere." I stubbornly stick to my theory. "The RV is gone, so that's proof the family is gone."

"Check their social media for recent posts." Becca gestures to Leo's phone. "They might have let fans know where they're performing."

"Good suggestion...here's their Facebook page." Leo scrolls down. "You're right, Becca. They posted about a performance at a graduation party. They replaced a band in Fresno that canceled."

I'm pleased to be right—it doesn't happen often with Leo—but I'm disappointed too. If Lyric had Trixie, then my bunny was safe. But if Trixie escaped on her own, she could be lost in the woods and bushes along the river. The wind is whipping fiercely, and the darkening sky warns of an impending storm.

If Trixie is lost outside, how long can she survive?

I'm ready to leave for home, but Leo has other ideas.

He opens his drone case and takes out the tiny dragon drone. "I will demonstrate my upgraded Dragon Drone 4.5," he explains. "The camera now swivels 360 degrees, allowing video to be filmed from all angles, including upside down."

Curious, I come up beside Leo. He places the dragonfly-shaped drone on his hand. His palm is up like a launch pad. Slim metal wings whoosh into the sky and whirl over our heads.

Leo gestures to Lyric's home. "Want the drone to look through the windows?"

"What's the point?" I ask with a discouraged shake of my head. "Lyric isn't home, and she probably left yesterday. She didn't steal Trixie, so it's not right to spy on her home."

"But I want to test out my drone," Leo explains.

"How about the garage?" Becca points to a rectangular building behind the house.

"I guess that would be okay." I shrug. "It's probably just cars and tools."

Leo pushes a knob on the remote and the drone whirls over a fence, over the empty driveway, and beyond the peaked roof of the house. The metal bird grows smaller and smaller until it's just a tiny dot in the sky...and then it sinks into the shadow between the house and the garage.

"I can't see it anymore," I complain.

"Watch here." Leo points to a tiny screen on the

control panel. It's like watching through the eyes of a real dragonfly. The screen shows sky then walls and a window. "Now for some aerobatics."

The view through the window is foggy. It's dark inside the garage, and I can't see much except vague shapes.

"I'll activate the Eyes Bright function. I boosted the drone's infrared vision." Leo adjusts a lever and a stream of light shoots from the dragonfly's eyes.

"Coolness," Becca says, peering over Leo's shoulder. "I see a truck, crates, a ladder, and a refrigerator. Your drone is amazing, Leo."

"It's basic robotics," he says with a shrug. But I can tell he's pleased.

I smile to myself. Leo is so smart and such a good friend. And I'm suddenly sad because he might move away. Why does he have to go visit that dumb school for smart kids anyway? If he moves in with his father, I'll hardly ever see him. And when he invents new drones, he'll show them to his new best friend Riley. She'll have suggestions for improvements and work with him to build more robots. They'll spend so much time together people will give them one name like *RiLeo*.

"You look so sad," Becca says, squeezing my

hand. "Worrying about Trixie?"

I blush, not wanting to admit my real thoughts. "I've never stopped worrying about her," I say, which is mostly true.

"She'll be okay," Becca assures me. "We'll keep looking."

"Well, she's obviously not here. Let's go to my house and search again." I glance up at ominous dark clouds. "If she's lost outside, we have to find her before it rains."

"Poor little thing must be so scared." Becca nudges Leo. "Put your drone away so we can look for the bunny."

"Sure, sure," Leo says, distractedly. "Hmm... that's odd."

"What?" I follow his gaze to the tiny screen.

"I just saw something. No, it had to be a mechanical error." He maneuvers the controller then taps on the screen. "There it is again!"

Becca crowds next to me. Our heads bump lightly as we bend over to peer into the screen. I don't see anything except a car hood—until I look past the car.

Two fiery orbs glow in the darkness.

Ghost eyes.

- Chapter 15 -
Lady Bell

"I've heard of haunted houses—but never a haunted garage!" I gasp.

"OMG! A real ghost!" Becca grabs my arm. "I never thought I'd see one!"

"Me, either!" I stare at the drone video in disbelief. The lights glow like spying eyes—as if it can see us.

"You're both overreacting." Leo shakes his head like he's disappointed in us. "It is definitely *not* a ghost. The image must be an error. I'll bring the drone back and analyze the data. I'll prove the nonexistence of ghosts."

"Or discover that they *are* real," Becca says in a shaky voice.

Leo pushes a lever, and I lift my gaze to the sky. The tiny drone is a silvery dot against the darkening clouds. The dot grows larger as it soars over the house and slowly lowers to the ground by our feet. Leo scoops up the small drone, flips it over, and taps some buttons before he checks the controller screen.

"There doesn't seem to be a malfunction," he says in a puzzled tone. "But I assure you, whatever you saw was *not* a ghost."

"Then what was it?" I challenge, more curious than afraid. "Something spooky with glowing eyes is in that garage."

"Maybe the ghost was trying to send us a message?" Becca's voice rises with excitement. "It's probably boring being stuck in a garage. Maybe he wants to be friends."

"Or he wants us to help him," I say. "How does a ghost get trapped in a garage anyway?"

"Let's ask him." Becca grins. "I can make friends with almost anyone alive—and maybe dead too."

Leo looks at us like we're crazy. "Searching for something that doesn't exist is a waste of time."

"Only one way to find out for sure," I say, running toward the garage.

I hear footsteps behind me and glance over my shoulder to see Leo and Becca.

This is crazy, I tell myself. But a spy doesn't run away like a scaredy-cat.

Still, my heart thumps fast, and I don't want to enter the garage alone. So when I reach the side door of the garage, I wait for my friends to catch up.

"The door's probably locked." My hand wavers over the knob. But when I twist the knob, it opens easily. Too easily?

My whole body is one big goose bump as I follow Leo inside. He flips on a wall switch, turning scary shadows into ordinary things like a lawn mower, ladder, and dark-blue SUV.

"I don't see a ghost," Becca says.

"I told you the image was an error," Leo says.

"Could it have been a reflection?" I point to the large vehicle. "We probably saw the drone's light reflecting back in the headlights."

"False ghost alarm," Becca says with a relieved chuckle. "Nothing to be afraid of."

"I was never afraid." Leo strides over to the SUV. "But it wasn't a reflection from the car. The glowing eyes were beyond the car—over by that sheet."

I frown at the dusty gray sheet, which covers

something tall and narrow. It reminds me of the sheets we found draped over the leftover furniture when we first moved into our house. It's just a sheet, I tell myself.

Yet we all saw the glowing eyes...

"Maybe we should get out of here." Becca's voice quivers. "Kelsey! What are you doing? Don't touch that!"

But I grab a handful of sheet and yank hard.

Dust billows in a dark cloud, which makes me cough. When I'm done coughing and see what was underneath the sheet, I feel silly and laugh at my fears.

"Only a standing mirror," I say with a sheepish grin.

"At least we know what caused the shining image," Leo says. "The sheet is very thin. Look, you can see my fingers wiggle when I place it over my hand. The drone lights reflected in the mirror."

"And glowed like ghost eyes," I add.

"Exactly." Leo takes a handkerchief from his pocket and wipes dust from his fingers. "Fact proven: Ghosts do not exist."

At least not in this garage, I think, remembering the monstrous shadow I saw flash across a wall.

This garage may not be haunted, but I'm not so sure about my house.

"We're done here," Leo says. "We should go."

"Not without covering the mirror like it was before," I say, reaching for the sheet. As I toss it over the mirror, something metallic glints in a dark corner. "Leo, could you bring your phone light over here? I see something strange."

Dust puffs up and my nose tickles like I'm going to sneeze. Cobwebs shine silvery in Leo's light, and the dust is thick, as if no one has set foot here in a long time. Yet when I glance down, I see shoe prints. They're smaller than mine and lead straight to a metal box.

"It's a toolbox," I say, disappointed.

Becca tugs on my arm. "So let's get out of here."

Leo leans over for a better look. "A box that small would never hold all my tools. My tool cabinet is organized by size and function, and it takes up an entire wall. My favorite tool is a 6-in-1 reversible screwdriver because of its versatility."

I'm only half listening because I'm staring at the toolbox. I run my finger over the smooth metal lid. "There's hardly any dust—and what are these scratches?"

Becca leans closer. "Looks like writing."

"Leo," I call over to him. "Shine your light here."

Bright light reflects golden on the metal, and I run my fingers over the scratched lettering. L-I—no, a Y—R… "*Lyric!*" I cry. "The toolbox is hers!"

"It's not unusual for someone to store a box in her own garage," Leo points out.

"I can sense a secret when I see one," I say excitedly. "Why else would the box be hidden? And the footprints prove that Lyric was here recently."

"What are you waiting for?" Becca's ponytail brushes my shoulder as she leans close. "Open it!"

In the shine of Leo's phone light, I flip up the latch…and groan.

"Drats. Nothing exciting." The top tray is divided into cubbyholes full of hooks, lures, and fish bait. "A boring tackle box. Gran Nola has one like it, except hers is red."

"Those shiny pink balls are pretty." Becca points to a small jar. "What are they?"

"Salmon eggs."

"They're used for bait," Leo says.

"Eww." She wrinkles her nose. "Gross."

"Says the girl who cleans up animal poop every day," I tease.

"That's different." Becca grins.

"Hmm, what's underneath?" I wonder.

When I lift the tray, I expect to see another tray with fishing equipment. Instead, there's a tiny silver figurine of an old-fashioned woman.

"Ooh, pretty," Becca says. "Much better than fish bait."

"Unusual fishing accessory," Leo murmurs. He shines his phone closer, the silvery statue shimmers like it's alive.

"Wow! She looks really old!" The figurine fits into my palm and feels surprisingly heavy. The woman has short bobbed hair, a curvy chest, and a gown that covers her legs.

Something shifts underneath the skirt. A bell chimes, and the sweet sound vibrates through my fingers. When I flip over the full skirt, booted legs sway.

"She's a bell!" I hold her by her silver head and enjoy the musical chimes.

"Coolness!" Becca exclaims. "Her legs are bell dingers."

"They're called clappers," Leo corrects. "This statue appears to be an antique. Kelsey, may I examine it?"

I hold his phone light while he studies the bell.

"Fascinating," he murmurs, rubbing his finger over some symbols beneath the skirt. After he returns the bell to me, he takes back his phone and taps the screen.

"What are you googling?" I ask, squinting in the dim light.

"Bells," he answers then pumps his hand in the air. "Found it!"

"Tell us," Becca urges.

"This figurine is called a lady bell," Leo says, reading from his screen. "Bells like this were once used by wealthy people to call a servant into a room. The most valuable bells have leg clappers and were made in Russia."

"So she's worth a lot?" Becca asks with rising excitement.

"If this dates back to the eighteenth century, it could be worth over a thousand dollars."

"Wow!" Becca reels back, banging her elbow against the mirror. "Ouch!"

"Leo, can you tell the difference between fake and real silver?" I ask.

"Not without running a test," he replies. "Silver is not magnetic. I could determine the authenticity if I were at home and could test it with a strong magnet."

"But we can't take it." I shake my head. "It belongs to Lyric."

"Does it?" Becca's dark brows rise in doubt. "It's weird to find an antique in a tackle box."

"Not that weird," I argue. "She has a lot of siblings like I do, which makes it hard to keep secrets. I have to keep my notebook of secrets and my spy pack hidden so my sisters don't find them."

"But why hide a pretty antique? I can only think of one reason." Becca puts her hands on her hips. "I know you like Lyric, but I don't trust her. She seems shady. I think she stole the lady bell."

I shake my head, wanting to defend Lyric. But doubts cloud my thoughts. I count the evidence against her.

She asked me not to tell anyone we met.

She said she'd come to my house but never did.

She hid a valuable antique in the bottom of a tackle box.

And I wonder, could something else be hidden there? I dig back into the box. Beneath spools of fishing line, bubble gum, round red bobbers, and a photo of a large fish on a pole, I find a folded blue paper.

I pick up the square of blue. Why does it look so familiar?

I unfold it and see spidery handwriting—just like the clue Lyric showed me that said to "Follow the bunny."

But this clue is even more mysterious.

Beneath the light of Leo's phone, I read six words:

STARE UP TOO FOUR THE PRISE

- Chapter 16 -
Clueless

"It's not like any clue I've ever seen," I tell my club mates as we ride to my house a short while later. Before we returned the blue paper and lady bell to the tackle box, Leo snapped a photo of the clue. I've read it at least fifty times and am even more confused.

"The grammar and spelling are incorrect," Leo adds as he rolls between our bikes.

"I wonder if Lyric ever solved it." My tires crunch on the gravel road leading to my house.

Becca flashes me an uneasy glance. "Are you going to ask her?"

"And admit we snooped in her garage?" I sigh, confused not only about the clue but also about friendships. Is Lyric even my friend? What will I say to her when I see her again?

"You don't need her assistance to decipher this clue." Leo smiles at me. "You have excellent cryptography skills."

His praise makes me feel warm inside, but I'm not sure I can do this. "It doesn't make sense. It seems more like wordplay, maybe a riddle. We're supposed to stare up at something—or maybe *four* somethings. But what? Stare seems to be the key word, but there are no directions to say where we should look. Probably somewhere in my house, since that's where Lyric wanted to 'follow the bunny.'"

"That's assuming the two clues are connected," Leo points out skeptically.

Becca nods. "This could be an old clue that has nothing to do with Lyric's prize."

"We won't know until we figure it out," I say.

"The misspelled words disturb me." Leo frowns at his phone. 'Too' should be 'to,' and prize isn't spelled with an *s*."

"Mistake or clue?" I wonder.

As our wheels thump-thump across the wooden bridge, I mentally scramble and rearrange the letters. *Ripesoot? Stupper? Ratter? Spare? Freaps?*

Letters tangle in my head like a tornado, leaving me dizzy and more confused than ever.

"Maybe it's only part of a clue," Becca says as she holds her wind-blown ponytail down, "and we're missing something important."

"We sure are," I nod, my heart heavy as I park my bike in front of my house. "We're missing Trixie."

"Don't give up hope." Becca puts up her kickstand and wraps me in a hug. "We'll keep looking until we find her."

Smoke-gray clouds darken the sky, and a sweet smell warns of rain. Fierce winds batter us as we look everywhere for Trixie—including the hidden berry-patch tunnel leading to the river. When I reveal this secret trail to my friends, Becca decrees it "coolness." And Leo actually kneels down on the dirt to crawl through the tunnel.

We spot a few wild bunnies, but there's no sign of our sweet little lop-eared.

I feel miserably hopeless.

Is she even alive?

When the sky rips open with rain and we're frozen like human popsicles, we reluctantly give up.

After Becca and Leo go home, I work on the printed copy of the clue that Leo made for me.

I consult my codebooks, but as I suspected, it doesn't match any clue patterns. It has to be a riddle, only with just six words, it's impossible to decipher.

There's a knock at my door, and I shove the paper under my pillow.

Dad steps in, dark circles ringing his eyes as if he hasn't been sleeping well. His gaze drifts over to the empty rabbit cage then back to me. "Any news?" he asks.

"I wish." I hang my head. "I looked and looked and looked. My friends helped too…but she's gone."

"I'm sorry, Kelsey." Dad sinks to the edge of my bed. "It's not your fault."

"But it is! When I heard someone in the house, I carried my cat out of the room but left Trixie. I don't know if someone has her or if she's lost outside." I swallow a salty taste like tears.

"We may never know what happened." Dad's shoulders sag. "But I have a responsibility to uphold. That's why I can't wait any longer."

I look up at him uneasily. "For what?"

"To call Mr. Dansbury," Dad says in a heavy voice. "He needs to know that the bunny he trusted in our care is gone."

"No! Don't tell him yet!" I grab Dad's hand. "I'll keep looking for Trixie."

"It's been over two days. She isn't coming back." He gives me a sorrowful look, and he leaves the room.

The thud of the door closing behind him sounds so final, like coming to the end of a story only to find out that everyone dies.

I scoop up Honey, bury my face in her fur, and the storm inside me bursts.

The tears I've been holding back stream down my cheeks.

I will never see Trixie again.

🐾

Things get worse the next morning.

When I get to school, Becca is waiting for me at my locker. She's twirling her ponytail anxiously, and her expression is darker than a thundercloud.

"I got a text from Danielle," she blurts out.

"Only one?" I try to lighten the mood. "You and your cousin are constantly texting about the fund-raiser."

"This is serious." Becca groans. "Danielle says a storm is predicted for Saturday."

"So?"

"Wags and Wash is being held outside the animal shelter," she points out. "Rain means it'll have to be canceled!"

"All I see is sunshine." I gesture out a nearby window where golden sun shines high, as if summer has arrived a month early.

"But a storm is coming. Weather is *so* stupid." Becca stomps her sneaker. "I have over two dozen volunteers coming to wash dogs—and now rain might ruin everything!"

"Weather reports can be wrong. The storm might fizzle out."

"That's our only hope." Becca sags against a locker. "Danielle makes her final decision tomorrow morning. If the forecast still predicts rain, the fund-raiser will be canceled. Cross your fingers and hope for sunshine."

We try to be positive, so every time we pass in the halls, we lift up our crossed fingers and say, "Think sunshine!"

My sunshiny, positive thoughts are dampened, though, when Tyla stops me in the hall after lunch. She's in diva mode today.

"Becca told me the dog wash might be canceled."

She clicks her tongue in fake sympathy. "That's *so* tragic. I'm *so* sorry."

She sounds so *not* sorry.

"Nothing has been canceled yet," I snap. "It may not rain."

"Then why does the weather report predict the biggest storm of the year? It's too bad." Her coiled braids seem to slither as she shakes her head in fake sadness. "Now we'll never know which of us would have won the challenge."

"Seriously? That's what you care about?" I demand. "The goal is to earn money for the animal shelter, not to win a dumb challenge."

Tyla's ruby-glossed lips rise in a smile. "Then you won't mind losing."

"The only ones losing are the dogs." I grit my teeth to control my temper. "If it rains, there won't be a fund-raiser to save them."

"Yes there will—just not your fund-raiser," she says with a smug lift of her chin. "The Sparklers will help those poor unfortunate dogs, rain or shine. You know what they say—the fund-raiser must go on!"

No one says that, and her little cheerleader gestures are just annoying.

"What are you talking about?" I raise my voice to be heard over the noisy kids streaming around us in the hallway.

"Washing dogs has to be done outside because it's so messy." Her snarky smile widens. "But transforming plain dogs into glamour dogs can take place anywhere. So the doggie spa is moving from the animal shelter to the rec room at my father's golf club. It'll be hard work, but I will save animal lives." She talks like she's a martyr offering herself as a sacrifice.

"I really need to get to my next class." I try to move around her but she blocks me.

"I just wanted to let you know that Becca won't have to choose between our fund-raisers," she says. "Becca will volunteer with the other Sparklers."

Becca already chose the CCSC, I almost say. But I bite my tongue. While it's obvious Becca, Leo, and I hang out together, our club is a secret.

"And because I'm so generous, you and your volunteers won't be left out," she continues in a tone sugary enough to rot teeth. "You're invited to help beautify dogs too."

"That's kind of you," I say sarcastically.

"I believe in passing on kindness." Her mauve fingernails sparkle as she presses her hand over her heart. "It's my goal to improve and save lives."

"By painting dogs green?" I roll my eyes.

"Not just green—sapphire, rose, lemon chiffon," she says proudly. "Fortunately, hard work doesn't have to be messy or boring. My fund-raiser will have refreshments and a live band. After each dog is glamorized, I'll give their owner a signed photo of myself posing with their dog. Also, we'll play videos of the unfortunate shelter dogs that need homes. Dogs will be adopted, and we'll make so much money that the shelter can buy *two* mobile pet vans."

Her fund-raiser will be a huge success—which is great for the shelter. I should be happy about this, but Tyla is like a thorn in my foot that keeps jabbing me. Maybe it's selfish, but I want the CCSC to earn the money to save the dogs.

Please don't let it rain! Not only because of the fund-raiser, but because of Trixie too.

Dad may think she's gone for good, but I'm still hopeful. She's probably lost and is trying to find her way home. But a storm could make that impossible.

When I get home from school, I search for her again. All through the house, the garage, and the yard. But still no sign of the tiny floppy-eared bunny, and I finally have to give up.

That night, I fall asleep repeating "think sunshine" and wake up early to clear skies and a shimmer of sunshine through my window. I don't usually watch the news before I leave for school, but I'm anxious to hear the weather forecast.

And a miracle happens.

The storm has stalled. No rain until Sunday!

When I hear the phone ring, I don't have to be psychic to know it's Becca. We squeal excitedly and discuss plans for the fund-raiser. With more than twenty eager volunteers, it's going to be the most amazing dog wash in the history of dog washes! And the shelter will soon have a mobile pet van.

I practically dance into school. And when I pass Tyla in the hall, I flash my biggest and most confident smile. I don't care which of us earns the most money for the shelter. It's all about saving dogs. After school, Becca and I are going to the shelter to help Danielle set up for the fund-raiser. Leo can't come because his father is taking him to Socrates Smarty Pants School.

As Becca and I roll out of the school yard, she suddenly points to the street.

"Isn't that Leo?" she asks.

I follow her gaze to a blond boy opening the door of a sporty red car with a familiar middle-aged man behind the wheel.

"Yeah." I watch him place his gyro-board into the backseat. "He said his dad was picking him up."

"So who's the girl?" Becca asks.

A tall black-haired girl steps out of the passenger seat and goes over to Leo.

Riley, I guess. Her long shiny hair flows around her shoulders. And the smile she gives him is way *too* friendly. She gestures to the front seat, but Leo shakes his head, always so polite and unselfish. It's too far to read his lips, but I know he's offering to let her sit up front.

She opens her arms and hugs Leo—like she's his girlfriend!

When Leo slips into the back, she scoots in beside him.

And they drive away.

After hours of organizing buckets, brushes, hoses, and dog shampoo, we're ready for our big day tomorrow. It's dark by the time I get home. I'm exhausted and just want to crawl into bed. But as I enter the house, I sniff sweet and sour Chinese food and my stomach grumbles.

"I knew you'd be late." Dad steps out of the kitchen, holding a covered dish. "Sit at the table and I'll heat it up."

"Thanks, Dad. Sorry I missed dinner, but there was a lot to do. I can't believe how much work goes into washing dogs!" I tell him about our preparations for the fund-raiser while I dig into a plate of stir-fried noodles, mushrooms, chicken, rice, and an egg roll.

"Impressive. I'm really proud of you, Kels." He ruffles my hair. "It's great to see you working so hard to help animals."

"I can't let those dogs die."

"That's my girl." He leans over to kiss my cheek. "I'm donating to the cause too. I made peanut butter dog cookies that you can take tomorrow for the dogs. I'd bring them myself, but I won't be there as early as you will."

"You're coming?" I say, pleased.

"Your mom and I wouldn't miss it! And not just us," he adds with a wink.

As I twirl my fork in noodles, Dad pours himself a cup of coffee and sits beside me. A storyteller at heart, he describes his day as castle chef. His employer, Mr. Bragg, had unexpected guests who were vegan, so Dad had to change his dinner menu. "No time to go to the grocery store, so I went outside to the garden. I pulled vegetables and wild weeds like clover," he adds with a laugh. "They said it was the best salad they'd ever tasted!"

Dad laughs. He's in such a good mood, I hate to ruin it. But I've been wondering all day how Mr. Dansbury took the news about Trixie.

So I take a deep breath then ask. "Was Mr. Dansbury angry when you told him Trixie was missing?"

"Um…no." Dad gets a strange look on his face. "We had a good talk. He was glad I stopped by, because he'd wanted to see me."

"Why?" I frown, thinking of the lost bunny flyers I'd put up and the online posts on missing pet sites. "Did he already know about Trixie?"

Dad shakes his head.

I wrinkle my brow. "Then why did he want to see you?"

Dad takes a sip of coffee before answering. "He gave me a gift."

Now I'm really confused. "But why? It's not your birthday."

"It's not just for me; it's a generous gift for our whole family," Dad adds, reaching into his pocket. "Apparently it's a tradition for his realty office to give a thank-you gift to clients after the purchase of a new home. Look what he gave us!" Dad fans out six tickets in his hand. "Tickets to *The Princess Bride*—the hottest musical in San Francisco. It's been sold out for weeks, so we're really lucky to have tickets."

"But what about Trixie?" My mouth hangs open. "Doesn't Mr. Dansbury care that we lost her?"

"Well...not exactly." Dad glances away as he sets the tickets on the table. "Because...well...he doesn't know."

I almost spit out my noodles. "You didn't tell him?"

"How could I? He was so nice to give us the tickets. It wasn't the right time to bring up such a sad story. But I will tell him..." Dad blows out a coffee scented breath. "In a few days."

"But Dad..."

"Tomorrow is going to be a big day, Kels," he continues in an upbeat tone. "Your dog wash is going to be an amazing success. And afterward the Case family is going to a musical. I can't wait to tell your mother. She's going to be excited!"

I wish I could be excited, but the CCSC still has mysteries to solve, including Lyric's clue. And I'd hoped Becca and Leo could come over after the fund-raiser. But will Leo even want to come over? Or will he have plans with Riley? Did she convince Leo to enroll in her school?

With so much on my mind, I toss and turn in bed that night. Dreams drag me into a maze of berry bushes, and I'm trying to find Trixie, but thorny vines wrap around me like ropes. I struggle and cry for help, and suddenly Leo appears. As he reaches out to rescue me, he transforms into a dark shadowy creature with large floppy ears and teeth as sharp as knives...

I jerk up, trembling.

Glancing over at my sisters, I'm relieved they're still sound asleep.

I'm careful not to wake them as I tiptoe over to my dresser to get my copy of Lyric's clue. I creep over to the closet, slide inside, and shut the door.

Feeling around for my spy pack, I unzip it and take out my flash cap. With one click, a light shines on the paper.

STARE UP TOO FOUR THE PRISE

Wordplay is usually fun, but there isn't much to work with here. "Stare" and "prise" seem important like they are key words. But what do they mean? And why are "prise" and "too" misspelled?

Shifting to a more comfortable position, I read the clue backward: Prise the four too up stare. Nope, still doesn't make sense. I try fixing the grammar, taking away an O and swapping *s* for *z* so it reads correctly: Stare up to four the prize.

That isn't any better, but something about this sequence triggers an idea. Why are only two words spelled wrong? Is it a hint for how to solve the clue?

Just like that, it hits me.

I know where to look for the treasure.

- Chapter 17 -
Wag and Wash

In the morning, I wake to marshmallow clouds drifting across a clear blue sky. The only hint that a storm is due tomorrow is a crisp wind that teases my ponytail.

There's no time to follow up on the clue since I have to get ready for the fund-raiser. My brother, who is working an early shift at Prehistoric Pizza, drops me off at the shelter. He gives me a twenty and tells me to donate it to the dogs. My brother is cool like that.

A huge sign on the animal shelter announces Wag and Wash Fund-raiser.

Hoses stretch from the building to a large grassy area arranged with chairs and tables. Busy volunteers set up shade tents and carry boxes. But I don't see Becca or Leo.

In front of the animal shelter, a bald guy with a tattoo sleeve carries dogs in cages to an "Adopt Me" booth. Many of the dogs up for adoption are the pugs that we helped rescue from a puppy mill. My grandmother adopted one of the pugs, a tiny big-eyed pup we named Buggy. But so many other dogs still need homes.

When Becca's cousin Danielle sees me, she puts me to work.

"Take a supply box to each washing station," Danielle says, gesturing to a stack of boxes of dog shampoo, towels, scrubbing brushes, and doggie treats. "Volunteers will work in teams of three—one to hold the dog in the tub, one to squirt the hose, and another to scrub the dog. Each station is set up with a washing tub, hose, and cleaning materials. I'll sign in the dogs and make sure they're friendly and don't bite so it's safe to wash them."

I nod, glad she's so organized. I have lots of experience washing Handsome, but I've never worked at a dog wash. I'm excited, but a little nervous too.

A few minutes later, I hear Becca's voice and see

her hurrying toward me. Her hair is tied back in a paw-print bandanna, and she's wearing worn jeans and a red T-shirt with a picture of a hairy dog and the phrase: *An outfit isn't complete without dog hair.*

"Finally!" I set down a box and throw my arms around her. "I've been dying to talk to you and Leo. Where is he?"

"On his way. He just texted." She points behind me. "Oh, here he comes now."

"About time," I say, ready to tease Leo for being the last to arrive.

But when I see who he's with, my smile fades.

Laughing beside him, as if he'd just told a joke, is the dark-haired girl he drove off with yesterday. She wears navy-blue overalls that look brand-new, and her hair is pulled back in two ponytails. Gold-rimmed glasses give her a chic nerd look. Maybe I should wear glasses...

"Riley," Becca guesses.

"Miss Smarty Pants," I grumble. "Why did she have to come?"

"Leo invited her. I was thrilled when he told me we had another volunteer." Becca gives me a startled look. "Don't tell me you're jealous?"

"Definitely *not* jealous." I fold my arms over my

chest. "It's just that I have CCSC news to share, and I can't talk around *her*."

Becca's dark brows rise. "What news?"

"I solved the clue." I lower my voice as I stare across the lawn. "But it will have to wait. Here they come."

Leo has a dopey grin on his face as he introduces Riley Chin. She doesn't smile, though, and moves close to Leo like she's his shadow.

"I am pleased to make your acquaintance, Rebecca and Kelsey," she murmurs, staring down at her blue high-top sneakers instead of looking at us.

"Same here," I lie.

"Coolness!" Becca is all bouncy cheerleader enthusiastic. "So happy you came. We really need volunteers. But my name isn't Rebecca; I'm just Becca."

"The diminutive for Rebecca is Becca," Riley says in a puzzled tone. "It's unusual for a nickname to be a full name."

"Mom didn't see any reason to give me a full name that everyone would shorten anyway." Becca chuckles. "And my name is the least unusual thing about me. Wait until you see where I live."

"On an animal sanctuary," I add proudly. "With

monkeys, raccoons, goats, horses, bears, peacocks, and even an alligator."

"Mom and I take care of abandoned and abused animals," Becca explains.

"Administering to disadvantaged animals must be highly fulfilling," Riley says.

"My life is never dull—that's for sure." Becca shares an amused look with me. "Last week, a monkey took Mom's keys and tried to drive the car."

Riley pushes up her gold-framed glasses. "Monkeys can't drive."

"Exactly," Becca says with a laugh.

Leo and I laugh too—but not Riley. Leo doesn't seem to mind, though, and leads her to the volunteer registration station.

More volunteers arrive: my sporty friends Ann Marie and Tori; Frankie with half the drama club; teachers Ms. Ross and Ms. Grande; and over a dozen kids from school.

Of course, the Sparklers stuck with their plan to set up their doggie day spa at a lah-de-dah country club, so they're not here. Tyla annoys me, but I want her fund-raiser to be a success. It's all about helping animals.

Danielle gathers the volunteers for group

assignments. I hold my breath when Leo's name is called. Please let him be with me, I think selfishly.

But he's grouped with Riley and Frankie. At least Danielle put me with Becca. The third person in our group is Mr. Thompson, the school janitor. He's a bearded teddy bear of a guy, and he offers to hold the dogs while we wash them.

While we wait for our first canine customer, I glance at Leo's group. Dramatic Frankie bounces around as he talks to Leo and Riley. With a streak of green in his hair, Frankie is the most theatrical person I know. He could describe his lunch and make it sound like a thrilling movie. Leo listens with interest, but Riley glances around nervously. And she's sitting *way* too close to Leo on the bench. When her gaze meets mine, her cheeks redden, and she turns away.

What's up with her?

No time to wonder, though, because dogs and their owners start to arrive and we're really busy!

There are so many dogs in all shapes and sizes, from a tiny teacup Chihuahua to a ginormous harlequin Great Dane. I'm reminded of a dog show I saw on TV, except most of these dogs are mixed breeds, and instead of being perfectly groomed, they need a bath.

Becca scrubs. I hose down soapy dogs. And Mr.

Thompson grasps the dogs firmly so they don't jump out of the tub.

I recognize many people that the CCSC has met while riding about Sun Flower looking for lost pets. One of them, a little girl named Emma, struggles to keep her scruffy dog Roscoe on his leash.

Suddenly she points at me. "That's the girl who helped find Roscoe!" she sings out to her parents. "I want her to wash my dog."

Unfortunately, Roscoe is a rascal and doesn't like baths. He squirms and wiggles so that more water gets on us than him. But no dog can escape Mr. Thompson's firm grip.

As we're drying off Roscoe, an elderly neighbor of my grandmother's, Greta, hobbles over on her cane with her large German shepherd.

"Major!" Becca tosses aside her rag and wraps her arms around the former search and rescue dog.

I drop my hose and rush over to Major too. The German shepherd is truly a hero. He's rescued other dogs and people too—including my mother.

Major obediently steps into the washing pool and sits patiently while we scrub him. If there were an award for Best Behaved Dog, Major would win it paws down!

Around us, the crowd thickens. Lines stretch long.

A woman in a long skirt passes out balloons and pamphlets on pet care. A puppeteer wanders through the crowds with furry animal puppets. And Aqua Man (a nice guy named Todd who loves dressing up for conventions) and his canine sidekick, Octo-Pup, delight kids by autographing their latest Octo-Pup comic book. There are refreshments, too—hot dogs and fries for the humans, and Dad's homemade dog treats for the tail-waggers.

The craziest moment is when Becca's mother gets into our line with a fuzzy ball of brown fur—not a dog, but a bear cub.

"I couldn't decide which of the dogs to bring, so I brought Fuzzy-Wuzzy," she explains with a grin.

"Cute little fellow," Mr. Thompson says, easing the cub into the water. He's careful with the burnt patches on Fuzzy-Wuzzy's skin. The poor little bear was orphaned in a forest fire.

"He's going to a zoo in Oregon soon," Becca's mom says cheerfully.

"I'll miss him," Becca adds. "But he'll be happier with other bears."

Mrs. Morales talks about the animal park while

we wash Fuzzy-Wuzzy. He loves the water and tries to drink from the hose I'm holding. We're having fun, and when I look around, I can see that everyone else is too. Now we just need enough money to buy a mobile pet van!

While we dry off Fuzzy-Wuzzy, Mrs. Morales offers to take us out for ice cream after the fund-raiser.

"Sounds yummy, but I can't." I shake my head regretfully. "My family is going to a play tonight." When I tell her it's a musical of *The Princess Bride,* her eyes almost pop out.

"That was my favorite book and movie as a child." She smiles wistfully. "I would slash the air with my toy sword and shout, 'My name is Inigo Montoya. You killed my father. Prepare to die!'" She laughs. "The musical has been sold out for months! How did you get tickets?"

"Our realtor gave them to us," I say.

"He must be a magician! Chad—I mean Sheriff Fischer—wanted to surprise me with tickets since my birthday is next week, but he couldn't get even one. That was very nice of your realtor."

"Well...yeah." But I feel guilty because he wouldn't be so nice if he knew we'd lost Trixie.

A few hours later, my arms ache from holding

the hose. I'm glad when we get a break, and I go over to the refreshment booth with Becca. We sit at a small table and squirt mustard and ketchup on our steaming hot dogs.

"Kelsey, I don't want to wait for Leo. I want to hear your news now. Please, please, tell me." Becca gives me a pleading look. "Or I'll die of curiosity."

"Well, I can't let you die." I grin. "I figured out the clue."

"The misspelled one?" She wiggles and almost knocks over the ketchup bottle. "No way!"

"Yes, way," I tease.

"What does 'Stare up too four the prise' mean?"

"It's the location of Lyric's prize. I think I know where, but it won't be easy." I lick mustard from my lips. "We'll need Leo's help."

Becca starts to rise. "I'll go ask him now."

"No!" I grab her arm. "We can't talk about CCSC stuff in front of Riley." I gesture across the grass to Leo's washing station, where he's scrubbing a large shepherd-mix dog. Riley stands so close to Leo her silky black hair brushes his shoulders.

"So I'll send him a text." Becca reaches for her phone.

"Well...that should be okay."

"Should I ask him to meet us at your house tomorrow?"

I nod but itch with impatience. "Too bad we can't search tonight."

"I'd love to—but you won't be home." Becca takes her last bite of hot dog and crumples the paper wrapper.

"Why did we have to get invited to a stupid play?" I groan.

Becca looks shocked. "How can you complain? It'll be super fun."

"I just wish it were another night," I say with a sigh. "All I can think about is the clue. I'd rather stay home. I have this weird feeling that time is running out if I don't search soon. And I can't search with my family around because the place to look is right out in the open. They'd ask too many questions."

"Not if they're gone," Becca says, with a sudden gleam in her eyes.

"What are you thinking?" I lift my brows.

"You don't want to go to the play, and I know someone who would love to take your place."

I follow her logic, and gasp. "Is that even possible? I mean, it would be perfect—but how can we make the adults do what we want?"

"I got this." A wicked grin spreads across Becca's face. "Here's what you have to do…"

- Chapter 18 -
Treasure Hunting

Hours later, Becca carries a small zebra-striped suitcase into my house.

I still can't believe her plan worked. When I first told my parents I wanted to stay home, their answer was a firm, "No way!"

But then I repeated what Becca coached me to say.

"It's not that I don't want to see the play. I really do—it sounds wonderful! And going with my family would be the best thing ever." I sigh like Becca suggested. "But I'm really tired after all that dog-washing today and want to sleep until tomorrow. Besides, Becca's mother really wants to go, only she couldn't get tickets. She's been like a second mother, and I owe her so much that I can't even list everything she's done for me. She has always been there whenever I needed help. This is my chance to do something nice for her. And next week is her birthday."

My parents' objections melted away.

Still, they were reluctant to leave me home alone while they're out of town, which is why Becca is dragging her suitcase into my room. We're having a sleepover.

Well, actually, a treasure hunting party.

And hopefully Leo will join us.

"Has he texted yet?" I ask Becca.

"Nope." Becca drops her suitcase on the side of my bed she'll be sharing. "But I'll text him again," she offers, taking her phone from her pocket.

"Ask him to bring his radar device," I say. "If my guess is right, we'll need it."

"You think there's another hidden wall panel?"

"There has to be. It's the only thing that makes sense."

"That clue is a bunch of nonsense," Becca complains. "I don't know how you figured it out. The misspelled words are annoying."

"But they're the key to solving the clue...in

reverse," I add mysteriously. "I'll explain when Leo gets here."

"His mother may not want him riding his gyro-board tonight." Becca gestures toward my window. "The sky looks ugly."

I go over to the window, pressing my hand against the chilly glass pane. Wind tosses the trees, and sunshine has been erased by a slate-black sky. Even with the window closed I can smell impending rain.

"We'll give Leo an hour," I decide. "Then we'll search without him."

While we wait, we create our own super salads for dinner. Dad left us with bowls of chopped chicken, bacon, cheese, and other salad toppings. He also baked oatmeal chocolate chip cookies and popped three different flavors of popcorn.

As I'm filling a plate with salad, Becca's phone dings with a text.

"Leo?" I ask hopefully.

Becca shakes her head. "Danielle."

"Drats," I mutter, sprinkling bacon crumbles on romaine lettuce.

Becca scans the text then grins. "Good news! Danielle says the dog wash was a success! Nine dogs were adopted, and we got lots of donations for a total of—" She taps her fingers on the table. "Drum roll, please! Twelve thousand dollars."

"That much?" My jaw drops. "But the math doesn't work. Most people donated twenty dollars—and we didn't wash *that* many dogs."

"There were some *big* donations." Her smile widens. "The largest came from your father's employer."

"Mr. Bragg? Wow! That's great!"

Dad had told me that wealthy Mr. Bragg's grandson RJ recently adopted an older cocker-shepherd dog that nobody else wanted. I saw them waiting in Leo's line at the dog wash. But I was too busy to do more than wave.

"What about the Sparklers?" I chop tomatoes for my salad. "Did their doggie spa make lots of money too?"

"Um...not exactly." Becca slips her phone back into her pocket.

I set my plate on the table. "What do you mean?"

"To quote Sophia, it was an 'epic disaster.'"

"What happened?" I drop my fork.

"Tyla hired a band to entertain people while their dogs were 'beautified.'" Becca makes quote signs with her fingers. "But the music was alt rock and so loud that dogs started barking and going wild. A huge mastiff got loose in the fancy golf recreation center, splashing purple paint and glitter everywhere—on walls, food, and people. A video was posted online and went viral. And 'glitter disaster' was trending on Twitter."

"Oh, no!" I gasp.

"It must have been so embarrassing." Becca blows out a soft-hearted sigh. "Tyla's father shut down the fund-raiser and told everyone to leave."

"How awful!" I feel sorry for the Sparklers, even Tyla. She annoys me, but we were working toward the same cause, and I'd hoped the fund-raiser would succeed.

"It's not all gloom and glitter-bombs," Becca adds more cheerfully. "Tyla's father donated five thousand dollars to the animal shelter. And on Monday morning, Danielle is picking up the mobile pet van."

"Yay for the van!" I lift my hand for a high five.

As we wash dishes, I keep my ears tuned for another ding from Becca's phone. But an hour passes with no word from Leo.

"He's not coming," I say as I try to put a plate on a high shelf. But I'm too short.

"Treasure hunting, party of two. We'll have fun searching anyway." Becca pats my shoulder, takes the plate from me, and easily slides it into the cupboard. "Unless you'd rather wait for Leo."

"Well...just a while longer. I'll tell you a story while we wait." I lower my voice dramatically. "A very scary story."

"Oooh! Fun!" Becca's dark eyes twinkle. "About the ghost bunny?"

"No," I shake my head, still freaked out about the long-eared shadow I saw. "This story isn't about an animal—it's about the little girl who used to live here." I make my eyes go wide. "Everyone thinks she drowned, but they're wrong. Want to know what *really* happened to Caroline?"

We set bowls of Dad's homemade popcorn on the coffee table, snap off the lights, and huddle on the living room couch in the glow of a candle. I think back to Philomena's storytelling and use my spookiest voice.

"It was a shivery, stormy night when Caroline heard bells ringing," I begin.

"Like the lady bell we found in the tackle box?" Becca grabs a handful of cinnamon popcorn.

"Dozens of lady bells," I exaggerate. "The sound

was so musical that it lured Caroline out of her bed. She was careful not to wake her friends—and left the room alone."

"Not alone," Becca reminds me. "Her bunny came with her."

"Oh, yes. The first Trixie was very loyal and followed Caroline into the...*Honey*!" I give a start when my cat jumps into my lap. I run my fingers through her soft fur, and she purrs.

"Kitties are loyal too." Becca smiles then gestures impatiently. "Go on with the story. What happened next?"

"The bells led her down the hall and to the staircase. The sound made the walls shake like the whole house was haunted."

And as I say this, distant chimes blow like a whispering breeze.

I tense. "Did you hear that?"

"What?" Becca looks around and shrugs. "Windows rattling?"

"No. Bells." I hold Honey closer. "There! I heard it again."

Becca touches her ears then shakes her head. "I only hear the wind."

Goosebumps crawl up my skin. "It's probably

nothing...just my imagination."

"The wind can make weird noises...what was *that*?" Candlelight flickers across Becca's wide dark eyes.

"What?"

"A thump." Becca's finger shakes as she points to the ceiling. "Upstairs."

I hold my cat close and stare upward. "But we're the only ones home."

"Are you sure?"

"Just us and the ghosts," I tease.

"We mustn't forget the ghosts," Becca plays along. "How many are there?"

"Dozens. That's why the room is so cold," I add with an exaggerated shiver. "Ghosts can't resist a good ghost story."

Becca laughs nervously, reaching for the popcorn bowl. "So go on with it."

"It might scare you," I warn. "Don't blame me if you have terrifying dreams."

"Oh, I'll blame you. But your nightmares will probably be worse." She leans forward on the couch. "So what really happened to Caroline?"

"Well..." I pause to think of what happens next. "Caroline followed the bells. And her bunny hopped behind her as she crept down the stairs."

"How could she see in the dark?" Becca asks. "Did she have a candle?"

"A flashlight." I roll my eyes. "Even Nancy Drew used a flashlight, and she solved her first mystery like ninety years ago. Caroline should have turned around, but she was too curious. She kept going down the stairs. When she reached the landing between the first and second floors, the bells rang louder—and the sound came from inside the walls. Turning to the wall, she saw something terrifying."

"A ghost!" Becca guesses.

"Worse than a ghost."

Becca gulps. "What?"

"The house was coming alive, and it was hungry for a victim." I sweep my hand around the room dramatically. "The wall along the staircase shifted into a skeletal face with giant jaws. The jaws snapped at Caroline. She was too scared to even scream. She tried to run away but the stair rails were long arms circling around her. And the stairsteps moved like a sideways escalator, carrying Caroline and her bunny closer to the wicked mouth of the wall. Caroline struggled to hold on to the rail. But little

Trixie was helpless, and a stairstep flung the bunny at the wall. Caroline screamed and called out—"

"Hey, is anyone home?" a voice calls out.

Becca and I scream.

Honey springs off my lap, streaking out of the room.

I jump off my chair, my heart racing crazy fast. "*Leo!*" I put my hands on my hips as I face him. "Why didn't you knock?"

"I did, but no one answered." He peers into the semi-dark living room. "Why did you scream? And what's the reason for a candle? Is the electricity out?"

"Kelsey was telling me a ghost story—until you freaked us out." Becca snuffs out the candle and switches on the ceiling light. "Why didn't you answer my texts?"

"I didn't see them until I got home." Leo pushes his blond hair away from his face. "My phone malfunctioned when a poodle tried to eat it."

"Poodles are a dangerous breed," Becca teases.

"You should have told us your phone didn't work before you left the fund-raiser," I say accusingly. "Or were you having too much fun with your *friend*?"

Leo scrunches his forehead. "Are you referring to Riley?"

"Who else?" I say sharper than I intend. "Did she ask you to enroll in her fancy schmancy school?"

"She mentioned it," he admits, glancing down at his black shoes. "It's a prestigious school that could be beneficial to my education."

"Humph." I fold my arms over my chest. "You'll move away, join a robot or coding club with her, and forget all about us."

"I could never forget. I have a nearly perfect memory."

Becca giggles. I shoot her an evil glare.

"But it's unlikely I'll sign up for extracurricular activities with Riley," Leo says.

"Why not?" I ask, surprised.

"She lacks a sense of humor." He looks directly at me. "She isn't fun like you and Becca."

Becca raises her fist. "Fun people rule!" At least I think that's what she says—her mouth is full of popcorn.

"So why did you hang around Riley like she was your new best friend?" I ask him.

"I was helping her overcome her social anxiety disorder. She's had private lessons her whole life and doesn't know how to converse with kids her own age." He pauses. "Talking to you and Becca terrified her."

"She's shy?" Becca pushes the popcorn bowl away. "I thought she was stuck-up."

"Me too," I add, feeling a little guilty.

"Riley is more comfortable around college professors. Her mother encouraged her to volunteer to improve her social skills. And my father asked me to watch over her." Leo sighs. "But I would have rather washed dogs with you."

"I wanted you with us too," I say, remembering when I first met Leo and thought he was annoying. But he's changed a lot, and so have my feelings for him.

Leo grins. "That's good because I've decided not to attend Socrates Academy—at least not this year. Instead, my parents are hiring a tutor for extra studying. So I'm staying in Sun Flower."

My heart twirls a happy dance, but I try to act cool and just nod. "Um...let's go treasure hunting."

"Why bother?" Leo scrunches his brow. "We already searched the house."

"Not that treasure." Becca gestures to me. "Kelsey solved Lyric's clue."

"You did?" Leo asks, sounding impressed.

"It wasn't that hard." I pull the paper from my

pocket. "I knew there had to be a reason why 'prize' and 'too' were misspelled. I played with the letters and words, but that didn't work until I realized the key to the clue was homonyms."

"Huh?" Becca straightens her leopard-spotted scarf.

"Look at the clue—'Stare up too four the prise.' A logical sentence would read either 'Stare up to the prize' or 'Stare up for the prize.'"

"Except we don't know where to look up," Leo points out. "There are no directions in the clue."

"There are if you change the key words into their homonyms. Prise and prize are homonyms. They sound alike but have different meanings. Too, four, and stare are also homonyms."

"So?" Becca shrugs.

"Prise wasn't misspelled—it was the wrong homonym."

Leo scratches his head. "I'm not following your logic."

"It's easier to show you," I say. "Do you have a pen and paper, Leo?"

"Always." He takes a pen from his vest pocket and tears a paper from a small notebook.

"To solve the clue, I have to change all the

homonyms. The only words without homonyms are 'up' and 'the.'" I write quickly then hold up the paper. "This is the homonym solution of the clue."

STAIR UP TWO FOR THE PRIZE.

"Stairs!" Becca points to the staircase, which winds up to the third floor.

"Stare is stair. Too is two. Four is for. And prise is prize." Leo tucks the pen back in his pocket. "Does that mean the prize is hidden under the second stairstep? And which floor?"

"I think I know," I say excitedly. "The clue Lyric showed me said to follow the bunny. And I remember Aunt Philomena saying Trixie liked to play on the stairs. When I let her out of her cage, she hopped down the staircase and stopped between the first and second floor. She looked up like she wanted to tell me something. Come on, let's find out."

I hope I'm right, I think, crossing my fingers as we hurry to the staircase. Trixie already led me to the hidden panel in my turret bedroom. Is the memory of her leading me to another one?

Since searching is dirty and spiders might be involved, I go into the kitchen and get three sets of plastic gloves. Then our treasure hunting team gets to work!

The staircase curves up to the second floor, turns, and continues on to the third floor. Trixie always went to the stairs between the first and second floor, so that's where we go.

The staircase must have gleamed golden a long time ago, but now the wood is chipped and stained. Refinishing the staircase is at the top of my parents' repair list.

We kneel on the second stair, and I feel around it for a button, knob, or indentation.

"Try lifting it up," Leo suggests—and it works!

But there's only a thick layer of dust inside.

"Nothing," I say, disappointed.

Becca points upward. "Maybe it's the second step on the next floor. We can go up and—"

Thump. The sound echoes from upstairs, followed by a shrill animal cry.

"That's Honey!" I jump to my feet. "My cat's in trouble!"

- Chapter 19 -
The Cat's Clue

"It came from the turret room! Let's go!" I race up
to the third floor, taking the shortcut up the spiral
staircase instead of the main staircase. Footsteps
pound close behind.

We find my orange kitty pawing the turret
room door.

My heart thuds as I scoop her up. She squirms to
get out of my arms, but I hold on tightly. "What's
wrong, Honey?"

Becca points to the closed door. "She wants
inside."

"Why?" I say, puzzled. "It's just an empty room."

"Appearances can be deceiving." Leo lowers his
voice. "You already discovered the key in the hidden

panel. And we all heard the thump. Someone could be in there."

"Or *something*," I add uneasily.

He crosses his arms over his vest. "I hope you're not suggesting the presence of a ghost."

"I hope I'm not either." I shudder.

Becca presses her ear against the door. "I only hear the wind. Maybe the window blew open."

"A logical theory," Leo says approvingly. "It was so windy when I rode here that I nearly fell off my gyro-board."

Hugging my cat, I stare at the door. "We should check inside."

"Yeah," Becca agrees. But she doesn't move and neither do I.

"Inactivity achieves nothing." Leo twists the knob and the door yawns open to reveal...

An empty room.

Yet something feels wrong. I study the broken window that rattles as each burst of wind blows through the jagged crack. The only piece of furniture is an old wood chair that's lying on its side near the window seat.

"Brrrr." I wrap my arms around my shoulders. "It's cold in here."

Becca looks around nervously. "Rooms are cold when there's a ghost."

"Or when the glass on the window is cracked," Leo points out. "The thump we heard was probably the wind knocking over the chair—an act of nature—nothing supernatural."

"So why is my cat so spooked?" Honey squirms out of my arms and springs onto the window seat. Swishing her tail back and forth, she paws at the lid of the window seat and mews.

"She wants to get in the window seat," Becca says with a wide-eyed glance around the room. "What's scaring her?"

Leo rolls his eyes. "Nothing."

"It's okay, Honey," I croon softly as I scoop up my kitty and hold her tight. "It's just a window seat."

"Should we open it?" Becca asks.

I frown. "It's probably full of spiders and cobwebs."

"Or mice," Becca says. "Cats have strong hunting instincts."

"A good reason *not* to open it," I say as Honey struggles to escape my arms. "No mouse snack for you."

I start for the door, and Becca follows. But Leo stares down at the window seat. "I-I heard something just now...something larger than a rodent." He points. "Inside there."

He grasps the curved metal handle and yanks hard.

The lid opens to a flash of red hair.

And someone screams.

- Chapter 20 -
Sound of Music

"Stop screaming!" I shout at the trembling girl huddled inside the window seat. "Lyric, what are you doing here?"

"I-I didn't...I mean..." Her eyes flash fear. "You startled me."

"You startled *us*!" I accuse.

"Um..." She hangs her head and her red braids sway against her knees. "Kelsey, I can explain."

"Tell me the truth," I warn, my tone cooler than the storm brewing outside.

She jerks up with a shake of her head. "I wouldn't lie."

I snort. "You said you would come over, but you didn't."

"That wasn't my fault. I had to go with my family."

"And now I find you hiding in my house? I should call Sheriff Fischer."

Becca gestures to her pocket. "I'll call him."

"*No!*" Lyric grasps my arm. "Please, don't! I didn't do anything wrong."

Leo frowns. "Breaking and entering, possibly with the intent to steal, is clearly a crime."

"And bunny-napping," I snap. "You wanted to follow my bunny, then both you and Trixie disappeared."

Her mouth falls open. "Trixie is gone?"

"As if you didn't know." Becca points to Lyric. "Don't fake innocence. Where did you hide her?"

"I didn't know she was gone." Lyric climbs out of the window seat, brushing off dust and plucking a cobweb from her braid. "Kelsey, I'm not a thief. Yeah, there's stuff I didn't tell you. But I'll tell you now—just do *not* call the sheriff."

I purse my lips. "Nobody else had a reason to steal Trixie."

"I didn't do it." Lyric grasps my hands. "How could I when I was with my family? And I figured I'd come over when I got back—that's why I'm here today. But when I got here, your car was pulling out of the driveway. I thought everyone was gone."

"So you broke in," Becca says sharply.

"The back door wasn't locked. I couldn't resist looking around." She twists the end of her braid. "I was on the stairs when I heard voices in the kitchen. I freaked out and hid in here."

"Why didn't you wait so we could search together?" I demand.

Her pale skin reddens. "I'd already waited so long—two years. And if I found the prize, I would have told you later."

"Like you told me there was a second clue?"

Lyric's hands fly to her freckled cheeks. "You know about that? How?"

"We went to your house, looking for you," I say. "No one was there, but we thought we saw something in your garage—and found your tackle box."

"And you're calling *me* dishonest?" she cries angrily. "You snooped in my personal things!"

"And you pretended to be my friend so you could search my house!"

"I never pretended—I really like you." Her eyes cloud with tears. "But now you hate me and think I'm a thief."

"If you aren't, then where did you get that lady bell? And why hide a valuable priceless antique in a tackle box?"

"Mrs. G gave it to me. She said it might be part of the rumored treasure. But she was afraid treasure rumors would spread again."

"Why not tell me about the second clue?" I purse my lips.

"I was embarrassed because..." Her voice cracks. "I couldn't figure it out."

"Neither could I," Becca admits in a friendlier tone.

"But Kelsey solved it," Leo says with a proud look at me.

Lyric's green eyes widen. "You did?"

"I like figuring out puzzles," I say with a modest shrug. "But we haven't had a chance to search yet."

"Let me search with you. Please," Lyric begs.

I want to trust her, not only because she could help us follow the clue, but because she's my closest neighbor and it would be nice to be friends. "Well... it *is* your prize. But you have to be completely honest with us."

"I will!" Lyric says with a heavy sigh of relief.

"I've been waiting to search for so long. Finally, I'll find my prize...and maybe more."

"What do you mean?" I close the window seat and scoot between Becca and Leo on the edge of the seat. Chilly wind blows through the window, and I lean closer to Leo.

"Mrs. G said music echoed all over the house, as if the walls were alive," Lyric says.

Becca gives me a startled look. I know she's remembering my ghost story. But it was just something I made up to scare her...I hope.

"Mrs. G seemed so excited...I didn't know she was sick." Lyric's shoulders slump. "She couldn't wait for me to follow the clue and hinted that I'd find *real* treasure."

"But you said she didn't believe that treasure existed," I remind her.

"She didn't—until she found it. Actually, Trixie found it." Her soft laugh is heavy with sadness. "Mrs. G said I'd have to solve the clue to find it, and she gave me the clue you saw in my tackle box. But I couldn't solve it. What was I supposed to stare at? Why was prize spelled wrong? I asked for another clue, and Mrs. G gave me one. But following Trixie didn't help and only made Mrs. G really tired. She told me she

needed to rest and asked me to come back later..."
Lyric's green eyes cloud over. "And I never saw her
again." Tears stream down Lyric's cheeks, and Becca
slips her arm around the younger girl. I feel bad for
calling Lyric a thief. If the last gift from someone I
loved was hidden, I'd break rules to find it too.

"We'll find your prize," I assure Lyric, then
explain about homonyms stare-stair and too-two. I
also show her the hidden panel in the turret room.
"See that black smudge?" I bend down to point.

Lyric peers closely. "A paw print."

"A painted bunny paw," I say. "Watch what
happens when I push it."

The small panel slides open, and Lyric "oohs!"
in delight.

"This must be where Mrs. G found the lady bell,"
I say. "Trixie led me here."

She wrinkles her brow. "But this isn't where she
hid my prize."

"Not unless Mrs. G left you an ugly old key and
stale rabbit food," I say, closing the wall panel and
turning back toward Lyric.

"She only gave me cool gifts." Lyric's smile is
bittersweet.

"Like the lady bell?" Becca guesses.

"Best gift ever. It was for my tenth birthday."

"Did she say where she got the bell?" I ask.

"No, but she said something odd." Lyric knits her brows. "When I thanked her, she told me to thank the house."

"So she must have found it here!" An idea jumps into my head, and I point to the hidden panel. "Trixie showed me this panel, so she probably showed Mrs. G. And there must be another hidden panel by the staircase!"

We're a parade of treasure hunters, hurrying down the stairs. My heart soars as I imagine a pirate chest gleaming with gold and dazzling jewels. But first we have to find it.

"I don't see knobs or buttons on the wall or rails." I run my hand over the faded railing.

"The stairsteps are hollow." Lyric grasps the edge of a stairstep and lifts. She peers into the hole and puckers her face. "Only dust and...eww!"

Still, we look inside every step leading up to the first floor. And Becca and Leo do the same with the second and third floors. But we all report a big fat nothing.

"I was so sure the clue meant to look there," I say, pointing. "There's no place else to look."

"We need Trixie to lead us," Lyric says sadly. "I miss that cute little bunny."

My heart hurts, and I'm so discouraged I want to cry. "There's nothing else we can do," I say, listening to the wind howl fiercely, as if the storm is in a hurry to get here. "I hate to give up, but Leo and Lyric should get home before it rains."

Leo nods.

But Lyric kneels down and reaches into the second step.

"We already looked there," I tell her.

"But we didn't look under the dust." She rubs her gloved hand around the inside of the step. "I thought I saw something…oh, just dirt stains."

"There are stains all over this house," I say with a heavy sigh.

"But these are perfect black circles," Lyric says.

"Circles?" I shine the flash-cap light on four small black spots. "A painted paw print!"

"Exactly like the one upstairs," Leo adds, excitedly.

Lyric's brows rise. "So all I have to do is press it?"

"Do it!" Becca urges.

I stare at Lyric's small hand. She stretches out her finger and presses…and nothing happens.

"Well, it was worth a try," I say.

"Wait!" Lyric cries. "I felt something move."

"Try again." Leo leans forward. "Press harder."

Creak!

Stairs rumble beneath our feet. Panic surges through me as I flash back to my dream of the house coming alive. But panic changes to excitement when a crack slices down the wall and a panel slides sideways to reveal a gaping doorway.

A secret passage.

- Chapter 21 -
The Walls Are Alive

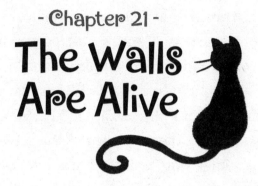

We gape at the wall that has become a narrow doorway, stretching from floor to ceiling.

Leo steps forward. "We should proceed with—" Dust puffs from the hole, and he coughs. "—caution. I'll go first to assess the safety level."

"Okay, but wear this." I take off my flash cap and offer it to Leo. "The light is stronger than the one on your phone."

His fingers brush mine as he grasps the flash cap. Then Leo plunges into the dusty darkness.

I hold my breath until I hear him call out, "I see no obvious risk. You may enter."

I step through the hole, and Becca and Lyric follow close behind.

I wrinkle my nose at the dank, musty odors. It smells as if no one has been here for a very long time. The flash cap shines across a small room the size of a pantry. There's no treasure chest, only a narrow wood table. I blink when Becca clicks on her phone light and nearly blinds me.

"Lower your phone, Becca," I say. And when she does, I notice the door behind the table.

"Another door!" Leo grasps the old-fashioned brass knob, but it's locked. "I have my spider key in my pocket."

"No need to pick the lock," I say, recognizing the shape of the keyhole. "The key I found in the turret room should fit."

"My prize!" Lyric suddenly cries from behind us.

I spin around as Lyric lifts a foil-wrapped box on the table.

Dust makes me cough. I cover my mouth with my hand. A silky cobweb brushes my face, and I swat it away. Leo and Becca shine light on a gift tag. "*For Lyric.*"

Lyric unties a silver ribbon and opens the red gift box. She reaches inside and withdraws a small brass statue with a full bell-round skirt.

"Another lady bell! And a note, too! It's Mrs. G's

handwriting." Lyric chokes a sob. "Kelsey, read it...please."

"Okay," I say softly, then take the paper and read out loud:

My dear Lyric,

Congratulations for solving the clue. Now you know my secret!

I found two hidden panels while chasing after Trixie. The other is high in the turret and holds the key to the door behind you. It's a tunnel with steps too steep for me, so I don't know what's down there.

If you're brave enough-and I know you are!-you'll find out. This may be our last adventure as the doctor warns my heart is slowing down. I love you like the granddaughter I never had and can't wait to discover this secret together.

"But we never did," Lyric says sadly.
I slip my arm around her. "You can do it now."
"We'll help you," Becca adds warmly.

"Wear this." Leo offers Lyric the flash cap.

"But I need the key to open the door," Lyric says.

"Not a problem," I say. "I'll go get it from my room."

I gulp a big breath of fresh air when I leave the dank room. I practically skip up the stairs—I'm so excited. We found the second passage! And we may find the treasure too.

I'm imagining a pirate chest full of gold coins when I hear an odd sound from the second floor. I freeze in place. Slowly I look down the hall toward my bedroom.

Something moves...a shadow flickers across the wall.

My bedroom door creaks open and then closes.

OMG! The shadow monster is in my room!

I start to run away until I remember that last time I saw the shadow no one believed me. If there really is a ghost, I need to see it for myself.

So I creep down the hall, grasp the knob, and slowly open the door.

- Chapter 22 -
Confronting a Shadow

I couldn't be more shocked if I saw a ghost. Actually, I'd rather see a ghost, because that would make more sense.

What is our *realtor* doing in my room?

And why is he holding my bunny?

"Mr. Dansbury!" I shout at the sweating middle-aged man. Instead of his usual neat shirt and tie, he's dressed in all black.

"I would normally say I'm glad to see you." Mr. Dansbury's shoulders sag. "But I find myself in an awkward position. I have no idea what to say."

"Start off with why you stole Trixie!" Fury rolls off me like a heat wave. "You gave her to us then took her away."

"I didn't mean to…" His voice trails off.

"I didn't know if she was dead or alive, and I have been sick with worry!" I glare. "Why would you do such a horrible thing?"

"It's complicated," he says miserably. "I don't think someone so young can understand."

"I understand all right—you broke into my house and stole my bunny!"

"I didn't plan to take her, and technically I didn't break in," he says with a guilty flush. "I have a key. It's an extra I found recently, and your father asked me to drop it off at your house when I was in the area. Here, take your bunny." He holds out Trixie to me. "I'll explain everything."

He doesn't seem dangerous—just embarrassed. Cautiously, I grab Trixie then step back in the doorway. Trixie makes squeaky happy sounds and nuzzles her nose against me. I hug her then aim a warning look at the bunny thief.

"You should know that I'm not alone." My voice shakes. "My friends are downstairs. They're taller and stronger and have phones to call 911."

"You have nothing to fear from me," he assures me, wiping sweat from his balding head. "I only came back to return the key and Trixie."

244

I snort. "As if I'd believe that."

"It's true. Your arrival has been quite a shock, and I'm a little dizzy. May I sit down?" He gestures to a chair by the rabbit cage.

"Well...okay." I stay in the doorway, poised to run.

"A few days ago when you visited my great aunt, I was in my office," he says. "The door was open, so I overheard you and Aunt Philomena. She told you what happened when I was young and accepted a dare to stay the night in this house."

"You got scared and ran home," I say.

"I'm not proud of my actions." His shoulders sag. "It was a stormy night—like tonight will be soon. I didn't believe in ghosts, but I believed the rumors of treasure. I wanted to impress my buddies by sleeping in a haunted house and finding treasure. So I spread out my sleeping bag and fell right to sleep...until I heard bells."

"You're not the only one," I can't resist saying.

"That doesn't explain why you took Trixie," I say accusingly.

He clasps his hands in his lap. "I heard you tell my aunt the bunny would lead to treasure. And I remembered Mrs. Galano—she was a dear friend—saying

Trixie had a habit of sniffing out hidden places. I couldn't stop thinking about the treasure, wondering if it really existed. I had to find out." He clears his throat. "So I borrowed Trixie."

"Stole her," I retort, hugging my bunny.

"I didn't mean to," he pleads. "After I took Trixie out of her cage, I heard someone inside the turret."

"Me," I say. "Short day at school."

"I almost had a heart attack, I was so scared."

"You were afraid of *me*?" I ask in surprise.

He nods sheepishly. "I waited until you were in the kitchen, then hightailed it out of there."

"Through the back door," I remember with a shiver. "Your shadow looked big and scary like a long-eared monster!"

"No one would ever call me big or scary. I was always the small, wimpy kid at school. And my ears are small." He touches his ears. "I was holding Trixie, so you must have seen our combined shadows. I suppose a nerd—even a grown-up one—and a bunny can cast a spooky shadow. Sorry if I scared you."

"I guess we scared each other."

"Still, there's no excuse for my bad behavior," he says with a deep sigh. "I wanted to return Trixie, so

246

I came up with a plan to sneak Trixie back into her cage. But this time I made sure the house would be empty."

A thought clicks in my head. "That's why you gave my family the play tickets."

He nods. "It wasn't easy getting them, either. I know someone involved with the theater who helped me get the tickets. I felt good about my plan. Your family would enjoy a wonderful play and come home to find Trixie back in her cage. No harm done."

"Except I gave my ticket away and stayed home." I shoot him a suspicious look. "Why not just tell my parents the truth? Unless you wanted the treasure for yourself."

Instead of looking ashamed, he laughs. "I may not look like it, but I'm a wealthy man. I have zero interest in the treasure—except to prove that it exists. My pride is more valuable to me than money."

The funny thing is that I believe him. It's the kind of corny thing my dad would say.

"Now my reputation will be ruined." Mr. Dansbury groans. "Decades of hard work destroyed because I ran away. Again. I'm so sorry. Please forgive me."

"My parents will probably be mad." Trixie nuzzles my arm and looks up at me with shining dark eyes. "But I'm just glad Trixie is safe."

"I owe your parents an apology." Mr. Dansbury takes a deep breath. "But I would like to be the one to tell them what I've done. No more running away."

He sounds so miserably ashamed that I feel sorry for him.

An idea pops into my head. "Before you confess," I say, "I have a question."

He tenses, as if afraid of my words. "What?"

"Would you like to look for treasure?"

After double-locking Trixie in her cage and retrieving the key from my spy pack, I lead Mr. Dansbury down the stairs. He gasps when he sees the doorway in the wall. "But this wasn't here when I came up the stairs. Astonishing! And to think it's been undiscovered for all these years!"

"Until Trixie led Mrs. G to it," I say proudly.

We step through the hole. My friends stare in shock at the realtor. I quickly tell them that Mr. Dansbury brought Trixie home. It's the truth, just not all of it. I'll tell them the rest later. This moment is about treasure hunting, and I don't want anything to ruin it.

"Lyric, here." I hand her the old key.

"Turns out an ugly old key is a great gift," she says excitedly. "I can hardly believe this is happening!"

She pokes the key in the lock.

Rusty hinges creak, but the door doesn't budge until we all get together—even Mr. Dansbury—and shove. The door creaks open. A staircase plunges into a pit of blackness. Musty odors cloud the air, and my eyes water.

"Go on, Lyric," Becca urges. "If you need more light, you can use my phone."

Lyric taps the flash cap. "This shines enough light."

"Yeah." I add. "Find the treasure like Mrs. G wanted you to." Lyric disappears like a magic trick into the darkness.

Becca illuminates the small room with her phone, so I don't miss the look Leo gives me. It's excited, nervous, and hopeful. I reach out to grasp his hand. Smiling shyly, he entwines his fingers into mine. And I smile too.

I'm not sure how much time passes, but finally I

hear the soft thud of footsteps.

"She's coming back!" I rush forward to peer down the staircase.

A bright light flashes. Lyric rushes into the room. Her face is dusty, and her green eyes shine. "You have to see this!" She gestures toward the stairs. "But be careful—some of the stairs are broken."

The steps are slippery and a few are missing, so we move cautiously. Becca stumbles once, but Mr. Dansbury catches her. The narrow passage twists and turns deep inside—maybe even under—the house. As we near the bottom, I hear the musical trill of bells.

Lyric shines the flash cap on a cellar-like room with cobwebs, crumbly cement walls, and chilly air that gives me goosebumps.

And in the center of the room is a tall wooden cabinet with a broken glass door.

As we're standing there gaping, a swift gust of wind sweeps from the high-beamed ceiling and bells tinkle softly, harmonizing into an eerie chorus.

The glass cabinet door hangs open, revealing shelves of bells, crystal and china glassware, and a few silver-framed photographs. Some of the bells are mounted on hooks and sway back and forth.

"Astonishing!" Mr. Dansbury exclaims. "I've never seen so many antique bells."

"I was hoping for jewels," Becca says. "But the bells are coolness."

"I wish Mrs. G could have seen this," Lyric sighs.

"She must have suspected what we'd find since she'd found the two lady bells." I pat Lyric's shoulder. "She said you were brave enough to come down here—and she was right. She'd be proud of you."

Lyric flashes a freckly grin. "I'm proud of me too."

The wind stills and slowly the chimes fade to silence.

"Congratulations, young lady." Mr. Dansbury pats my hand. "If your family decides to sell the cabinet and its contents, it'll bring in a tidy sum."

"My family?" I ask, surprised. "But Mrs. G wanted Lyric to find it. Her clues led her here."

"I love my lady bells, and I'll treasure my note from Mrs. G forever," Lyric says. "This adventure was her last gift to me—it just took two years to unwrap it."

Mr. Dansbury turns to me. "Kelsey, everything inside this house—including this cabinet—belongs to the Case family." His voice no longer sags with shame, but rings with realtor confidence.

"Wow!" Dollar signs dance in my head.

"I'm familiar with fine antiques," Mr. Dansbury says, brushing dust off the oak cabinet. "This cabinet is in good shape despite the drafty conditions. It appears to be a Hunzinger Merklen Quartersawn cabinet cupboard. If I'm correct, it's worth over $6,000. Not a fortune, but a nice start on the B and B renovations."

My head is spinning, and suddenly everything makes sense. "The bells only ring when there's a storm. The cabinet door is open, so strong winds make the hanging bells ring."

"That must be what Caroline heard," Becca adds with a shiver.

"Look." Leo points to a cabinet shelf. "A photo of Caroline."

I think of the photos Philomena and Sunflower Mary showed me and nod. This black-and-white photo was also taken at the last birthday party and shows two girls holding their stuffed bunny toys. I recognize Caroline and her best friend, Marjorie Ann, a.k.a. Sunflower Mary.

Leo picks up the picture carefully, blowing off dust. He tilts his head as if the gears in his brain are shifting through data. He returns the framed picture then snaps photos of everything in the cabinet.

As we file upstairs, the wind whips harder, and chimes clash chaotically.

The storm has come early.

Mr. Dansbury offers to drop Leo and Lyric off on his way home. Then he turns to me with a heavy sigh. "I'll come back tomorrow to talk to your parents."

A few hours later, I hear my father's car pulling into the driveway.

Becca and I jump off the couch and grab our jackets.

We rush outside into the rain shouting, "We found treasure!"

- Chapter 23 -
The Last Ghost Story

My family doesn't believe there's a treasure until we lead them through the hole in the wall, down the steep stairs, and show them the cabinet.

They're shocked and thrilled, and no one goes to bed until after midnight.

Becca and I wake up to the cinnamon smell of Dad's yummy banana bread. My parents look tired but happy and admit they couldn't sleep. They talked until morning and researched glassware and bells online, making plans to remodel our house.

"Of course, we'll put some money aside for each of you kids," they say.

But money is the last thing on my mind when Becca gets a text from Leo:

Noon @ Sunflower Mary

After breakfast, Mr. Dansbury arrives to keep his promise.

"I'm so glad you're here!" I rush forward and grab the realtor's hand. I pull him into the foyer and shout, "Mom and Dad! Guess who's here?"

Mr. Dansbury cringes. "Kelsey, please not so loud...this is difficult enough."

"Don't worry," I say as my parents enter the room. "I told them everything."

His face goes pale. "But I asked you to let me—"

I wave away his words. "That's not necessary. They totally understand."

"So the hero arrives!" Mom rushes over to hug the shocked realtor.

"Hero?" Mr. Dansbury looks like he's going to faint. "But I didn't—"

Dad pats him on the shoulder. "Don't be modest. First you give us tickets to the most amazing show I've ever seen, and then you search for Trixie until you find her wandering in a park. Thank you so much for bringing her back to us."

"You're thanking *me*?" Mr. Dansbury looks at me, and I wink.

"We're so happy to have Trixie safely back," I say firmly. "That's all that matters."

"But I…" He rubs his sweating forehead. "Oh, well…I'm glad too…and grateful."

He gives me a meaningful look, and before he can say anything else, I grab Becca by the hand. "We have to go meet with Leo."

"Yeah, right now," Becca says with a knowing smile. We'd had a long talk last night, so she knows what really happened with Mr. Dansbury and Trixie. Later, I'll tell Leo too, so the CCSC can officially close the case of the missing bunny.

The rain has softened to a light sprinkle after last night's furious storm. Our wheels slosh through the street, and water splashes our sneakers as we park next to Leo in front of Sunflower Mary's home.

"What's up?" I ask him uneasily.

He shows us a large photo of the two old-fashioned girls holding toy bunnies. It's the same image as the framed photo I saw last night in the treasure cabinet.

"I took a photo of the cabinet then enlarged the photo so I could examine details," Leo says with an excitement to his tone that hints of a big discovery.

Becca props up her kickstand. "And the reason why?"

"To solve the final mystery."

"What mystery?" I ask. "We know who took Trixie, and she's back home. We found the reason for the sound of bells—and a cool treasure. What else is left to solve?"

"A long-ago mystery. But first I need to talk to the only person who can confirm my theory." Leo gestures beyond the rain-sprinkled sunflowers to the house where an empty chair rocks slightly in the breeze.

Now I'm totally confused.

Sunflower Mary looks equally confused when she answers our knock. Leaning on a cane, she smiles. "Well I didn't expect to see you three back so soon."

"Us too," Becca says with a puzzled look at Leo.

"Ma'am, do you recognize this?" Leo holds out the enlarged photo.

"Of course. It was taken the day of the party." Sunflower Mary's mouth curves into a sad smile. "Where did you find it?"

"In a hidden passage," I can't resist saying.

"Oh, my! Now I'm intrigued. This photo brings back bittersweet memories." She runs her finger over Caroline's grinning face. "She was so excited that I had a toy bunny like hers. She dragged me over to the photographer and begged for a photo of us holding our 'twins'—that's what she called them. I loved my toy so much because it looked just like Trixie."

"But the toy bunnies weren't identical," Leo points out in his detail-focused way.

"Well, no." Mary shrugs. "The party-favor bunnies were made of cloth with glass eyes. But I didn't care. I loved mine because it was a gift from my best friend. Of course, it didn't last long, so I no longer have it."

"But you still have a bunny," Leo says with a challenge in his tone.

"I told you last time that I don't—"

"It's on your bed," Leo interrupts. "I saw it by accident when I was here last time. But you're telling the truth. It's not *your* bunny."

She stares at him for a long moment then sighs. "So you've guessed."

"Not everything," he admits. "I have some questions."

She crooks her finger at us. "Come with me."

As she hobbles to a back room, I wonder why Leo is so interested in an old bunny.

Just like Leo said, a small white and brown toy is propped up between pillows.

Sunflower Mary gently lifts it up and holds it out to me.

"The fur is so soft," I say, awed. "Just like the real live Trixie...well, *my* Trixie."

Becca leans over to rub the soft fur. "And the necklace sparkles like real rubies."

"That's because they are real rubies." Leo stares hard at Sunflower Mary. "Am I correct?"

The old lady's face sags. "Yes."

"But that would mean..." I gasp. "Is this Caroline's bunny?"

"I'll explain if you'll tell me about the hidden passage," Sunflower Mary says with a hopeful look at us. "I suspected Caroline's father collected something illegal or dangerous. What did you find?"

"Old bells," I say with a smile. "Not dangerous— but noisy on stormy nights."

"Bells? I never would have guessed!" Sunflower Mary throws back her head and laughs. "Yet it explains so much!"

I give the toy bunny back to her, and she lovingly returns it to the bed.

"Now I owe you a story," she says, then leads us into her living room. "Sit down and I'll tell you what really happened to Caroline."

"Is it a ghost story?" Becca asks eagerly.

"In a way," she answers with a wistful sigh. "Memories are ghosts of the past."

Becca, Leo, and I squeeze together on a couch while she eases herself into a reclining chair. She sets her cane aside and props a pillow behind her back.

"After the party, a few of us girls stayed over for a sleepover," she begins in a solemn tone. She's not a dramatic storyteller like Philomena. "We really did hear bells that night, but that's not why Caroline and I left the room. We both carried our toy bunnies, and Trixie hopped behind Caroline. I couldn't stop crying. Caro didn't keep any secrets from me, so I knew the plan."

"Plan?" I grasp the edges of the couch.

Sunflower Mary nods. "We crept outside to the waiting car."

"Caroline's mother," Leo guesses.

"You're right," the old woman says. "Her father had custody and refused to let them see each other. So Caroline's mother kidnapped her own daughter."

"And the bunny?" Becca asks.

"Yes. Caro wouldn't leave without Trixie."

I widen my eyes. "So Caroline didn't drown?"

"No, but the plan was to make it look like she had so that her father would leave them alone. Caroline was terrified of him, so I was happy she was escaping. But I was heartbroken to lose my dearest chum." Sunflower Mary sadly looks at the photo Leo gave her. "The plan was to leave marks in the dirt by the river's edge and a shoe to make it look like she slipped and fell in the river. The plan worked perfectly, and only I knew that Caro and Trixie were alive."

"But why do you have this bunny?" I ask. "Did Caroline give her to you?"

"No." She sits up straighter. "After Caroline left, I cried for weeks. It was easy to pretend she drowned because I missed her so much—and I knew I'd never see her again. Her mother wouldn't even let her write to me. Nearly ten years later I received a package with no return address. And when I opened it, I found—"

"This bunny!" Becca exclaims.

"Yes," she says softly.

"So Caroline wrote to you," I say happily.

But her face saddens, and she shakes her silvery head. "It was from Caroline's mother. She told me that Caroline never forgot me, even when she got sick from cancer and could barely talk anymore. But she found the strength to ask her mother to give me the bunny so I'd never forget her."

"And I've never forgotten her." She hugs the toy bunny to her chest. "This is more valuable to me than any treasure."

We're quiet as we ride back to my house.

We go up to my room and take Trixie out of her cage. We take turns holding her, and Honey meows to get some attention too. I feel like I've lost a friend, even though Caroline died long before I was born—even before my mother was born!

I glance over at my two best friends. Becca kneels on the floor, hanging her head upside down so Honey can swat at her pink-streaked ponytails. And Leo is flipping through a how-to-care-for-your-bunny book, probably memorizing every word.

And I start to smile, grateful to have such good friends. Before the CCSC, I spent most of my time reading spy books in my apartment. I felt lonely—until Becca, Leo, and I rescued three adorable kittens and formed a club. We're so different, yet we share a love for animals — and solving mysteries.

I jump up and grab my jacket. "Mom gave me some new lost pet flyers. Want to go look for them?"

"Great idea," Becca says.

"I'm right behind you," Leo says as we leave my room.

The air smells fresh from rain, and the sky is blue with cottony clouds.

Becca climbs on her bike, and Leo powers on his gyro-board.

I grin at my club mates, hop on my bike — and we ride off together.

About the Author

At age eleven, Linda Joy Singleton and her best friend, Lori, created their own Curious Cat Spy Club. They even rescued three abandoned kittens. Linda was always writing as a kid—usually about animals and mysteries. She saved many of her stories and loves to share them with kids when she speaks at schools. She's now the author of over forty books for kids and teens, including YALSA-honored the Seer series and the Dead Girl trilogy. Her first picture book, *Snow Dog, Sand Dog*, was published by Albert Whitman & Company in 2014. She lives with her husband, David, in the northern California foothills on twenty-eight acres surrounded by a menagerie of animals—horses, peacocks, dogs, and (of course) cats. For photos, contests, and more check out www.LindaJoySingleton.com.

100 Years of

Albert Whitman & Company

1919–2019

Albert Whitman & Company encompasses all ages and reading levels, including board books, picture books, early readers, chapter books, middle grade, and YA

Present

2017

The Boxcar Children celebrates its 75th anniversary and the second Boxcar Children movie, *Surprise Island,* is scheduled for 2018

The first Boxcar Children movie is released

2014

2008

John Quattrocchi and employee Pat McPartland buy Albert Whitman & Company, continuing the tradition of keeping it independently owned and operated

Losing Uncle Tim, a book about the AIDS crisis, wins the first-ever Lambda Literary Award in the Children's/YA category

1989

1970

The first Albert Whitman issues book, *How Do I Feel?* by Norma Simon, is published

Three states boycott the company after it publishes *Fun for Chris,* a book about integration

1956

1942

The Boxcar Children is published

Pecos Bill: The Greatest Cowboy of All Time wins a Newbery Honor Award

1938

1919

Albert Whitman & Company is started

Albert Whitman begins his career in publishing

Early 1900s

Celebrate with us in 2019!
Find out more at www.albertwhitman.com.